I0460781

The Soul Cache

The Soul Cache

Daniel MacKenzie

Published by Daniel MacKenzie

Copyright © 2015 by Daniel MacKenzie

All rights reserved. This book or any portion thereof
may not be reproduced or used in any manner whatsoever
without the express written permission of the publisher
except for the use of brief quotations in a book review.

Printed in the United States of America

First Printing, 2015

This is a work of fiction. Names, characters, businesses,
places, events and incidents are either the products of the
author's imagination or used in a fictitious manner. Any
resemblance to actual persons, living or dead, or actual
events is purely coincidental.

ISBN 978-0-9964203-0-3

Library of Congress Control Number: 2015911756

For those who keep searching

Chapter 1
Correcting Grammar in Suicide Notes

It was the feeling. The loss of control. The telling myself over and over again what had happened in an effort to make it fathomable. Why do some of the most real moments in life seem to be the least believable?

I first found out about Luke's suicide from our best friend Sarah. On the phone all she would tell me was that I needed to get to Luke's house right away. I can still hear the sound of her voice in my head, so full of horror and disbelief. She started crying when I pressed her to tell me what had happened. Had he been hurt? Was he dead? Deciphering no answers from her sobs, I eventually ended the call, got on my bike, and rode the few blocks to Luke's house. There was a police car on the street.

I dropped my bike on the lawn and ran to the front door. The main door of the Leary's house was open and I could see Luke's mom and dad in the living room through the screen door. Ripping it open, I marched right up to them. Luke's mom was sobbing into the arm of the couch while his dad stood talking to a police officer.

"Thank you, Rick," the officer said to Mr. Leary before turning and staring at me. "Are you..." he glanced at the notepad he was holding, "Owen Mitchell?"

"No," I replied as I looked at Luke's mom who,

overcome by sadness, remained unaware of my presence.

"I'm Eric," I said, returning my attention to the officer. "What's going on?"

"Eric Harrison," the officer stated looking back down at his small notepad. "I'm sorry to tell you this, but your friend Luke is dead. It appears he took his life earlier today."

I felt dizzy. The cop shifted uncomfortably as I continued to stare at him. Luke's mom had erupted in a new wave of tears having heard the officer tell me.

She was muttering something barely intelligible to herself. I looked over at her, trying to discern her words.

"I was caught up in that note, I couldn't stop focusing on the words," she babbled between fits of crying. "It's no wonder he's gone. It's all my fault! What kind of mother corrects the grammar in her son's suicide note?"

"He left a note?" I asked.

I felt a firm hand on my shoulder; Mr. Leary's face was expressionless.

"Where is Sarah?" I tried to ask calmly, but it came out as a yell.

"She's in the other room being interviewed by my partner," the police officer explained. "If you're able, I have a few questions for you as well."

"No," I replied defiantly, glaring at the cop. "I want to talk to *her*."

Luke's father tightened his grip on my shoulder.

"You should know, son," the officer began,

"that young lady was the one to find him. She's very," he paused for a moment, "distraught."

"I just need to talk to her," I insisted, shaking Mr. Leary's hand from my shoulder.

The screen door creaked and the sound of hurried footsteps followed. Owen appeared in the room out of breath.

"I got a call from Sarah. Is Luke okay?" he sputtered.

"Luke's gone," I answered simply as the officer referred to his notepad again.

"What?" Owen asked, looking up the stairs toward Luke's room where the three of us had spent many hours during our breaks from school.

Sounds of movement and of sliding chairs came from within the adjoining room and Sarah hurried into the living room. She was followed by another cop who stood in the archway as she ran and hugged Luke's father. Sarah comfortingly brushed her hand across Mrs. Leary's arm as she made her way to us. She embraced Owen and then me. Rivulets of mascara ran down her face and her eyes glistened with tears.

Sarah stood next to Owen and me in silence. The cop who had interviewed her was enormous. He filled most of the archway, and the attention of most everyone in the room was turned to him.

"I am sorry for your loss," he said in a deep voice. "There is a concerning matter in this young man's death," he continued, staring at Owen, Sarah, and me. "Luke left a note that mentions the three of you by name."

I felt sick to my stomach as he said this.

"Can we see it?" Owen asked, stepping toward him.

"Most of the letter addresses his parents and Madeline," the officer continued, not acknowledging Owen's request.

The name struck me. Madeline was Luke's kid sister who had died of cancer when she was just six. Did the officer even know this? What had Luke been writing to his dead sister? And why?

"Mrs. Leary has removed their section of the note and requested it remain private. However, Luke wanted you three to know this."

The officer handed Owen the bottom portion of the notepaper. Most of the page had been ripped off leaving only a few lines at the bottom. I peered over his shoulder to read it.

Sarah, Eric, and Owen:

Sometimes you can only find something when you really look, and sometimes it's hard to see what's right in front of you.

I watched from behind Owen's shoulder as he flipped the piece of paper over. We read the string of numbers that appeared on the back.

038 49 930 120 21 153

"A bit cryptic. Does this message, or the numbers, mean anything to you?" the officer asked. "Maybe some kind of code?"

I studied it for only a moment and knew. I looked up at Sarah who flashed the most subtle micro-expression that perhaps only years of friendship could allow me to pick up on. And even though nobody else in the room seemed to take any notice of our communication, her look gave me both a silent and resounding instruction: "Say, 'No.'"

"No," I answered. "Who knows what he was thinking? Clearly he was sick."

"Can we keep this?" Owen asked the officer.

"This note is evidence in our investigation," the policeman explained.

"But it's meant for us," Owen said confrontationally. "It refers to us by name." He pushed out his chest and stepped closer to the large officer.

The other officer was studying me with a hint of suspicion in his eyes. I looked away. Walking over to Owen, he took the note from his hands.

"Can we transcribe it?" Sarah asked.

Everyone in the room turned to look at her.

The officer scratched out the message on his notepad and handed the page to her like it was a speeding ticket.

"If you know anything that aids in our investigation, Luke's parents would be very appreciative that you share."

The three of us nodded.

"I recommend utilizing the counseling services at your school. Suicide is not an easy thing to deal with."

Sarah slipped the piece of notepaper into the pocket of her jeans as he said this.

Mr. Leary turned to the three of us. He was as composed and emotionless as his wife was hysterical.

"We will let you know when we determine the funeral arrangements. If you don't mind, we would appreciate some time alone," he said, nodding toward the door.

As we left, I heard a whimper from the den and noticed the Golden Lab puppy pushed up against the front of his kennel. It was Luke's dog, Rowdy, which he had adopted just a few months ago. Yet another life he had chosen to leave behind.

Chapter 2
Secret Numbers

I picked up my bike from the Leary's lawn and Owen and Sarah followed me to the sidewalk. Owen's black convertible was parked at an angle along the side of the road.

Behind Owen's car, I stared in a state of disconnect at the red cursive "California" written on the plate. My mind was trying to decide how to feel as I tightly gripped the handlebars of my bike.

"Leave your bike here, Eric," Owen instructed. "Let's go to my dorm."

I walked my bike up the Leary's driveway and rested it against the side of their garage as Sarah got into the passenger's seat of Owen's car. I squeezed into the back seat and Sarah slammed the door shut. The three of us just sat there with Owen holding the key still unturned in the ignition. Nobody said a word. Nobody cried. We just sat there. I stared up at the window to Luke's bedroom.

The rumble of the car returned me from my trance as Owen fishtailed onto the street and blew past the stop sign at the end of the road.

Sarah grabbed his arm. "So you want us dead, too?" she yelled.

Owen slammed on the brakes and I felt my seatbelt lock against my chest. The car remained motionless as Owen brought his hands to his face and started crying. I watched his broad shoulders shaking and Sarah still holding his muscular arm. It was strange seeing him cry.

"No, I don't want us dead, too," Owen snapped. "What the hell is wrong with you?" He glared at Sarah with his eyes full of tears.

Sarah let go of his arm and put her hands to her face. Now she was crying, too.

"At least you didn't find him," she cried.

Owen inhaled sharply and put his hands back on the steering wheel. He stared straight ahead at nothing as he asked the question.

"How did he do it?"

Turning my attention to Sarah, she was silent for some time.

"I found him hanging," she stared out her window, "by his belt."

I pictured the image in my mind. Hanging himself in the same room we built forts in as kids.

"I got him down. I don't know why. I guess I thought that maybe I could save him somehow," Sarah explained with disbelief in her voice. "And when I realized he was dead I called the police. Then his parents got home and I called you. His mom…she just lost it."

"Let's get to the campus," I suggested. I wanted to get as far away from the Leary's house as possible.

Owen drove at a more reasonable pace toward the university where he had just finished his freshman year. Luke had been his roommate. While their dorm remained open during the summer, Owen had elected to stay, but Luke had returned home.

Sarah and I had just graduated high school. She had dated Luke on and off the past two years. Life had been normal up until now. I was even excited for school to be over and by the prospect of going to the same college. But now everything was different. Everything was tainted.

Arriving at the dorm, Sarah and I jogged through the hallways behind Owen on our way to his room. Pausing just long enough for him to unlock the door, we spilled inside the cubicle-sized chamber which was dimly lit and half-emptied.

"Let's see the note," Owen said.

Sarah reached into the pocket of her tight jeans and struggled to slide out the piece of paper. She held the policeman's scribbling out to us. I reexamined the message the officer had hurriedly copied.

"They're coordinates," Sarah explained, pointing at the numbers.

Owen took the note from her with a puzzled expression. He stared right at it, bewildered.

"How do you figure?" Owen asked.

"It's the degrees and minutes," she explained further. "Luke probably left out the North and West and the decimals so that only we would know."

"Do you think he hid something here?" Owen questioned.

"Search that location on your laptop," I suggested.

Owen took a seat at his desk and opened the lid of his laptop.

"Come on," he commanded the computer impatiently.

Sarah and I silently stared at each other. I wondered what she was thinking; she was probably wondering the same thing about me. The only sound was the tap of Owen's quick typing.

"It's someplace in Eldorado National Forest," he stated.

"I've been there before," Sarah replied, breaking eye contact.

"How far is it?" Owen asked.

"Just about an hour and a half," she answered with emerging excitement in her voice.

"Well, let's go," Owen said, standing up.

Sarah was staring out the window at the sun's low point in the sky. Owen began busily throwing stuff from around the room into a backpack.

"Grab whatever you think we'll need," he instructed. "Let's plan on staying there for a while."

I grabbed a pillow and blanket from Owen's bed as Sarah opened the drawers of his dresser. Owen pulled a shower caddy from his closet and turned it upside down, emptying its contents into his bag.

"Let's get going," Owen said, herding us out of his room.

Together, we hurried out of the building to Owen's car. We threw the backpack and all that we'd grabbed into the trunk. Sarah had wiggled into the back seat this time, so I stepped into the passenger's seat. Sarah was looking at her phone. I studied her glittery pink phone case.

"Here," she said, passing the sparkly cell phone to me. "I put the GPS coordinates into my phone."

"It says we'll get there just before 8:00," I stated, looking at the arrow pointing its first direction.

Owen had already started driving. I set the phone on the divider between our seats.

Something about the road we were traveling on seemed to sober me to my situation. There was nobody else in sight. No traffic, no noise, nobody. Like the city had been abandoned. I was gripping my knees as the rumble of the car moved me slightly. There was nothing to do anymore. There was nothing I could do. All I could do was sit. That was my job. We were headed somewhere now. Luke was dead. And my mind was deciding for me that this was a time to try to process, a time to try to make sense of everything that had just happened, everything that was happening. I think Sarah and Owen felt it, too, because nobody was saying a word. Nobody was asking the new question that everyone was thinking: what are we going to find?

I thought about the suspicious look the officer had given me, and about the implication when he advised us to tell if we knew anything. Like we needed to confess something. But that officer didn't know Luke. He didn't deserve to know everything about him or his death.

Still, it was condemning. Something about having your name in a suicide note makes you feel like you did something terrible, or at least didn't do something you could have. My life with Luke was a good one. We were close. We had our occasional fights growing up, even drifted apart slightly once he went to college and I was still stuck as a senior in high school. But we didn't end on bad terms. I didn't cause his suicide. At least I hoped I didn't.

The sound of my phone ringing broke the silence. The screen showed the incoming call was from my parents. I hit "Decline" before turning off my phone.

"There's something that's just making me sick," Owen stated flatly. "It's this horrible *why*? All I can think about is, why did he do it?"

There was no reply from either Sarah or me.

"I mean, why didn't he talk to us first? Why didn't he ask for help? If I had just known what he was feeling, I could have done something," Owen insisted, glancing at the rear view mirror as if seeking Sarah's confirmation.

The sound that came from behind me lifted me from my seat. Sarah, the source of that inhuman shriek, now sobbed uncontrollably.

"He did talk. He talked to me!" she cried. "Two years ago, when we were dating, he asked me if I ever thought about suicide and if I thought there was even any point to living." Sarah wiped her eyes with her mascara-stained sleeve. "It's my fault that he's dead!"

Owen slammed on the brakes and, once again, the seat belts immediately cinched.

I stared fearfully at Owen as he turned around and glared at Sarah. Reaching his hand out toward her, he placed it on her knee.

"You are not the reason Luke is dead," he insisted in a firm voice that stressed every word.

Sarah let out a whine, still wiping her eyes.

"Have you?" I questioned Sarah through the rear view mirror as I wiggled to regain the slack in my seat belt.

"Have I what?"

"Ever thought about killing yourself?"

"Not really," she answered, switching arms to wipe her other eye. "Have you?"

"I don't know," I replied. "I've wondered about it before."

"I have," Owen interjected as he resumed driving. "I even held a loaded gun to my head. I was just so…" he stopped mid-sentence searching for a word, "mad," he concluded simply.

"About what?" Sarah asked.

"Everything. I felt like my life was a piece of shit. I was doing awful in school and my dad was being an asshole. I remember thinking that if I just pulled this trigger it would all end."

"Why didn't you?" I asked.

"Why didn't I?" Owen chuckled. "Eric, that's such a nice question," he said sarcastically, looking over at me and smiling.

I smiled back. It was the first attempt at humor since we'd heard what had happened and it felt different. It felt noticeable.

"You know what I mean," I replied. "What made you put the gun down?"

Owen laughed a bit at this. "I didn't want to

miss the TV shows that were going to be on that night."

Nobody said anything for a while as Owen headed toward the highway. The abrupt loudness of the woman's voice from Sarah's phone jolted us as she instructed us to merge. I had almost forgotten about our destination somehow.

"What's the ETA now?" Owen asked, staring straight ahead at the road.

I glanced down at Sarah's phone. "It's the same," I responded and felt Owen accelerate.

"What do you think is worth living for?" Sarah asked from the back. "When Luke asked me that, I didn't even think it was a question worth asking. I just thought it was some depressed thing to say, and that he would be back to himself the next day. Which he was, at least I thought so. But now I think maybe it really is a question worth considering."

"Friends, family," Owen began, "girls in bikinis."

"I'm serious!" Sarah laughed in unconvincing irritation.

"So am I," Owen responded with a faraway sigh.

Their exchange lightened my mood, and I was beginning to feel slightly grateful for this little journey. With all its uncertainty, it still held a destination and gave us a sense of purpose. In a way, it was helping. I was no longer stuck in that living room being interviewed by police and listening to Luke's mother's hysterical mutterings. I wasn't at home in my bed crying in confusion. Maybe Luke planned it this way. Maybe he thought that giving us this destination would help us cope with what he did.

"Alright, if you really want to know what I think," Owen began more seriously, "I think life does have meaning. I think it has the meaning we bring to it. Like Luke's art. Luke was an art major, you know? A bit of a stoner, and sometimes it was a pain being his roomie. But he seemed to get it. He'd pick up on things and his artwork was pretty cool. I think that's what gives life meaning."

The phone interrupted again and instructed us to continue on route.

"If he did hide something…" Sarah looked out the window at the sun creeping slowly toward the horizon, "I mean," she continued in a dreamy, distant voice, "if he left something for us to find, what if it's not there?"

"What do you mean?" Owen asked.

"Remember that summer, Eric, that we spent caching with Luke? Sometimes we couldn't find the cache. I mean, I get that it's supposed to be hard to find, but sometimes all three of us, searching and searching, couldn't find it even though we were right where the GPS told us to go. The accuracy is usually really good, too," she continued. "It usually got us within feet. But sometimes the containers get vandalized or people take them, or they get destroyed by animals or really bad weather. What do we do if that's the case? So much significance would just be lost. We'd never get to see the point of this."

"We're not even sure if this is a cache," Owen stated. "Or if those numbers are necessarily coordinates for that matter."

"I'm sure," Sarah stressed. "Especially with what Luke wrote to us."

"He might have just been talking about the point of living," Owen replied distantly, lowering his brow as though recognizing the disturbing connotation of what he had just said.

"Although once you see the numbers as a location, it is kind of hard not to see them like that. Well, anyway," he continued reassuringly, "we'll only start to worry if we for sure can't find anything."

As we drove, I stared out the window at a dead tree a great distance away that stood alone in a field. It appeared as though we would never pass it even as we sped along the highway. I let my forehead rest against the window. I tried to remember what the last thing I said to Luke was. It bothered me that I couldn't recall our final conversation. I wasn't even sure why I wanted to know so badly. Why it was that it seemed to matter so much. Really, it probably didn't matter. He would still be gone either way and remembering wouldn't bring him back. I considered it was probably something like "See you later." I cringed at that thought. Then another disturbing speculation went through my mind – I wondered if Luke knew what our last words were.

I continued watching the tree as we traveled.

"What about you, Sarah?" I asked. "What do you think is the point of life?"

"Well, I like what Owen said. But I think there's more to it than just what we bring. I mean, how awful would it be for people who can only live a life of suffering? I think that there's a bigger plan for things. Like, everything's connected somehow."

"Do you believe in God?" I asked.

"I don't know," she responded. "I mean, I want to, but I don't know. I guess I just believe in things mattering. What about you?"

"I don't know either, I guess. I'm not sure if I really believe in anything."

Owen was silent as he drove, but I could tell he was listening carefully to our discussion.

"Luke believed in God," he said, breaking his silence as the road became more mountainous. "We're getting closer."

"What happens if we get there late?" Sarah asked. "What if the park's closed?"

"Nothing's going to stop us from getting to those coordinates tonight," Owen insisted.

"What about darkness?" Sarah retorted. "I don't suppose you have a flashlight in that bag?"

"We can use our phones."

"It won't make a difference whether we find it tonight or tomorrow," I stated, attempting to eliminate any confrontation.

"I just need to know," Owen replied, glancing over at me with a look that showed some weakness around the edges of his otherwise sturdy demeanor.

The phone gave another instruction that I failed to hear. Hopefully, Owen was paying attention.

"Why here I wonder?" I pondered aloud as I stared at the now vast amount of green pines climbing with us up the rapid elevation.

"This place must have meant something to him," Sarah stated. "I mean, it is beautiful."

It was as if her declaring it beautiful made it so, as I took another look at our surroundings. The late-day sun was illuminating all of nature. The vast expanse of wilderness was untouched, undamaged, and still.

"This is getting steep," Owen announced as we felt the gears shift.

"There's the park sign just up ahead," Sarah said, pointing.

I glanced at the time on Sarah's phone – five before eight. Owen slowed the car as we approached the park entrance. He stopped next to the small station.

"Good evening," greeted a woman's voice, the source of which I couldn't see from my position in the car.

"Are there any campsites available?" Owen inquired.

"We're all full up unless you've got reservations," the park ranger replied.

Owen looked over at me as if for help – his lips were tight and his face was pale. It seemed like he might break down right in front of the woman. I leaned over Owen to speak to her.

"Do you know how long before there's an open site?"

"I can check," the woman replied.

"Can we just go hiking here?" Owen interjected. His voice was shaking.

The woman studied us suspiciously, glancing back at Sarah before looking upwards.

"Little late for a hiking trip, don't you think?"

For a moment I just wanted to do it. I just wanted to tell this woman our situation. Maybe she would understand. Or maybe she'd tell the police.

"It's alright," Sarah was saying quietly to us from the back seat. "We can just come back in the morning."

I saw a tear fall down the right side of Owen's face. He was staring down at Sarah's phone, which was still indicating our destination lay ahead. I watched as his eyes narrowed.

Awkwardly trying to wipe away his tear without the ranger noticing, he addressed her once again.

"Actually, I just remembered, we may have made reservations." His demeanor had changed as he resituated in his seat. Feigning confidence, he glanced over at me and then back at Sarah. His voice also had changed as he asked us with authority, "Can you remember whose name the reservation was under?"

The woman continued to study us as though she were going to ask what we were up to.

"Can you just check Owen Mitchell?" Owen asked in a frustrated tone, interrupting her silence.

The woman stepped back into the entrance station.

Putting his acting on hold, Owen turned to me for support.

"You think he reserved a camp for us?" I asked in disbelief.

I was interrupted by the park ranger's voice.

"Yes, Mr. Mitchell. I have you here for a three-night stay," she said as she reexamined Owen's convertible. "I just need you to sign this."

My heart was beating hard as I attempted to maintain my composure. Owen, all but paralyzed, managed to scribble a signature on the paper before handing it back to the woman.

"Enjoy your stay," the woman said in a half-skeptical, half-amused tone as she handed a pass to Owen. "You're in Camp 59."

We didn't talk to each other as Owen drove into the park.

Chapter 3
Death Lessons

Our tires churning the gravel roadway announced our arrival as we approached Camp 59. Owen stopped his convertible and Sarah grabbed her phone from off the divider between the front seats. We all stepped out of the car, sure that the reservation was all the proof we needed. Luke had hidden something for us to find here.

If the surroundings weren't sufficiently beautiful on our drive in, they were now. Our camp was near a great expanse of water. Sarah was reexamining her phone. I took in the sheer absence of smog, cars, and construction noise as I surveyed the majestic panorama. All those city nuisances had been replaced with ponderosa pines, mountain peaks, and bird songs. Dusty, speckled rays of light broke through the nearby trees. The day was leaving us.

Sarah's deep sigh caught my attention and I reflexively turned to her.

"Alright, it's nearby," she stated with an odd smile, looking up from her phone.

Owen and I peered down at the small screen. She pointed out the nearby destination indicator and the short line that connected it to our current location. Sarah looked up at the sky and her shoulders lowered. I imagined Luke watching us, enjoying this play out. Sarah pulled up the compass on her phone and pointed the way. She began running.

"It's less than a mile," Sarah called out as we jogged alongside her.

My heart raced with excitement. What were we going to find here? Maybe we would know why he did it. Maybe we would see why he arranged all of this.

There were other campers nearby as we ran. They started campfires and zipped up tents. Children giggled and parents scolded. All of them were people who had no idea…people who hadn't lost someone like we had; people who were fishing and didn't know what pain like this felt like; people with no clue what it's like to have someone close to them choose death over life – to hang themselves by their belt – and then to be left to try to make sense of that. To have to accept that.

We kept running behind Sarah, slowing only when she glanced at her phone and changed direction slightly. I intentionally breathed in the smell of the ponderosa pines and absorbed the rich vanilla aroma. It was as though I had to have some such sensory experience to continue existing; some sensation to feel real. I didn't analyze what I was thinking or feeling, but that smell was abundant and so I let it happen. I embraced the awareness as we ran.

Sarah stopped. Owen and I stopped behind her, gasping for air. We stared in the same direction as Sarah and saw the reason she had paused. The coordinates were about to lead us off the road. Standing there attempting to catch our breath, we peered into the dense forest.

"Well, let's go," I said with an edge of excitement. The shadowy expanse had a mysteriousness that was somehow inviting – as though the branches of the trees were beckoning us to enter. Sarah smiled at me and Owen nodded. We were soon trekking through the forest.

"It's supposed to be just up ahead," Sarah remarked, looking at her phone as she half tripped over a root.

Staring ahead, I struggled with doubt. I wrestled with the thought of how ridiculous our search would be if we were wrong. Like maybe we were only seeing what we wanted to see. That we had misperceived the numbers. That maybe we were all sharing some odd delusion to keep Luke alive to us a little longer. And that perhaps all we would find was a dead-end on this road paved with shared denial, a dead-end where we would all have to stop running and come to terms with this day from hell.

But there was the fact that Luke had reserved us a campsite here under Owen's name. There had to be something. I held onto that reassuring thought as we continued onward. And suddenly, she stopped. I almost ran into her.

"It's here," Sarah announced in a hollow voice, examining the ground around us.

I looked around, too, as though I were expecting some change in scenery to indicate its importance, but that would go against the idea of being hidden. Nothing about this place was different. It was just another place to get lost in the woods. Owen and I walked up to Sarah to reexamine the coordinates.

"It's 18 feet away," she stated, awkwardly taking steps in different directions while staring at her phone.

We shuffled next to her haphazardly before she declared, "Three feet."

It was eerily dark now, but the moon was providing some light for us. Sarah put her phone away. I bent down to examine our three-foot target. We searched in silence as the night noises began.

We didn't want to acknowledge the amount of time that passed, but Sarah eventually voiced what we had all been fearfully realizing.

"There's nothing here."

I could hear her give up in that statement. And at once I felt like I was standing next to her in Luke's room after she got him down. The moment she determined that Luke was gone; that he already had stopped breathing long before.

We stopped searching and all looked at the moon. Sarah fell to her knees.

"I just can't believe he's dead," she moaned. "What a coward!" She screamed to no one. "Just live. All he had to do was live!"

I sat on the uneven ground next to her to try to calm her down. Owen had stepped away from us.

"It's going to be okay," I tried to reassure her, and possibly myself.

"No, it's not, Eric," Sarah responded sharply.

"Luke's dead and I have to have that image in my mind for the rest of my life!"

I gripped her hand tightly, expecting to cry with her but I couldn't. The tears wouldn't come even though the pain was there. It was a horrible feeling not being able to cry, and I realized I had been the only one who hadn't. Maybe I felt like I needed to be the one to hold us together. I felt Sarah grip my hand back.

"What's this?" Owen's voice came from a short distance behind us.

Sarah quickly wiped her eyes and turned around. I got up slowly as I heard Owen's voice rising. "I think I found something!"

Sarah had stopped crying and crawled on her hands and knees over to him. He was kneeling. I crouched beside him, examining what he was looking at. He really had found something.

Sticking out of the ground, amongst the leaves and grass, was a sort of ribbon. Colored like camouflage, it flapped gently in the breeze. Together, in a blur of hands, we dug around the green and brown strip of cloth. As more of the dirt was removed, we found the ribbon to be tied to a wide golden ring. We dug faster, nearly scratching each other's hands in our haste. I felt the cool, moist dirt under my fingernails as we began to uncover the top of whatever the ring was connected to. It appeared to be the top of some kind of container.

Now further exposed, the object was shaped

like a large thermos, painted in the same camo pattern.

"I think that's enough," Owen said, sliding two of his fingers through the golden loop. He pulled up hard and the rest of the tube-shaped container slid out of its hiding place in the ground. Sarah and I scooted closer to Owen.

"You want to do the honors?" Owen asked, handing the container to Sarah.

"Alright," she replied, studying the object. She held it firmly with one hand and twisted the top with her other.

I watched her unscrew the top of the capsule. She placed the lid on the ground next to her and peered into the cache. My eyes never left her face as she did this, but her enigmatic expression gave me no clues as to the capsule's contents. Seemingly without emotion, she turned it upside down. Three large bundles of money tumbled to the ground, each bound with a mustard-colored currency strap labeled $10,000.

Grabbing one of the bundles, Owen fanned through the many hundred-dollar bills. "Holy shit," he stated in plain disbelief.

"There's also this," Sarah said, holding up a notecard.

"What's it say?" Owen asked, reprioritizing his gaze.

She held the note so that we could all read it.

Sarah, Eric, and Owen:

You found me.

The money is yours, but I want you to do something for me.
I want you to spend the night here at the campsite.

Tomorrow, at the intersection of Broadway and 9th, there will
be a homeless man. I want you to take him to dinner at Mer
d'Émeraude.

I'll be there.

"And, there's one more thing," Sarah stated
before any of us could react to the note. Reaching her
arm into the cache, she removed a small photograph.

Her face expressed mixed emotions as she
smiled weakly and passed the photo to Owen. Owen
put his hand over his mouth. I scooted close to him to
see the picture. It was a photo of Owen and Luke
standing outside their dormitory.

In the picture, Owen was posed with a clenched
fist and his arm pulled back as though he were going
to punch Luke, even though he was clearly laughing.
Luke was standing facing the camera smoking a
cigarette with one hand and giving the middle finger
to the person taking the picture with the other. I
looked at his blond hair and tattooed arms.
Underneath the photograph in black letters was
written: Be Kind.

Owen was chuckling as the memory took its
effect on him. His laughter proved contagious and
Sarah and I couldn't help but join in.

As our laughter subsided, we sat in silence. Then the night sounds of the forest were loud – louder than I had realized before. Buzzing from all around filled my ears and strange animal noises could be heard in the distance as bushes moved nearby.

"We should probably get out of here before the bears find us," Owen advised.

The coldness of the air was noticeable now, too. Returning to the campsite sounded like a good idea.

Sarah placed the bundles of money and the note back into the capsule and sealed it. Owen put the photograph into his wallet. He helped lift Sarah who was complaining that her foot had fallen asleep.

"Do you remember how to get back?" I asked, looking around and realizing I had no idea which direction we had come from.

"It's that way." Sarah pointed at knotted roots nearby without even pulling out her phone as she began limping through the woods. We walked beside her. I could feel our collective spirit had been lifted by finding Luke's cache. The relief of having been right about the coordinates. The thrill of the find. Hearing Luke's voice again in the note he'd written to us – even if only in my head. It was his voice, his words. Words newly expressed by him in spite of his death. Watching Owen react to the picture seemed to extinguish the blur of searing emotions leading up to the find. Now, it was like we were back to ourselves again; able to feel somewhat normal. And to complain about stupid, silly things like Sarah's foot falling asleep and walking too slowly.

"He wants us to take a homeless person out to dinner?" Owen asked, cracking up right after we had become silent again.

"I think it's sweet," Sarah replied somewhat defensively.

"Well, yeah, I mean it's 'nice,'" Owen began, "but it's just funny. It's just so Luke, you know?" Owen chuckled again. "It's exactly something he would do. Have us take some smelly drifter to the fanciest restaurant in town."

I laughed at this, thinking about how Owen was right; in some ways this was all "so Luke."

"I'm just wondering what we're going to find there," Sarah pondered.

"How do you think he got all this money?" I asked, thinking of the bills. "I mean he was poorer than I am."

Owen and Sarah didn't respond, and I worried I had said something terrible. Maybe it was my saying "was" because Luke will always will be referred to in past tense now.

"Sorry, should I not have said that?" I asked, suffering the continued silence of my friends as we continued walking toward our camp.

"It's fine, Eric," Sarah reassured, but I was not convinced. "I wondered that too. It just kind of makes me wonder if he saved up for this. Which makes me start thinking more than I want to about how long he intended this to happen; how long he had been orchestrating the events of his death."

Owen cleared his throat. "I considered all that, too, when I found out about the campground reservations. Luke did tend to plan out everything. That was one of the few ways in which he was responsible. And when I saw those empty campsites this late at night when we were running out of the loop," Owen continued, "I figured Luke probably made reservations for each of us just in case."

We broke through the last layer of trees and found ourselves back on the gravel road. The moon was a brilliant white.

"It's a full moon tonight," I announced.

Sarah stared in the direction of our campsite. "Well, he wants us to stay the night. Wish we'd brought a tent." She rubbed the sides of her arms for warmth.

"Nothing wrong with roughing it," Owen remarked. "We can sleep in the convertible. I'll put the top down so we can watch the stars. It'll be fun," he added, smiling down at her.

"Let's have a fire," I suggested, piggybacking on Owen's enthusiasm.

"Good idea! I'll get us some wood." Owen stopped in his tracks and turned back toward the woods. He hollered, calling out toward the trees as he ran, "I'll be back in a minute!"

Sarah and I arrived at the camp. We each took a seat on some large rocks that were near the rusted steel fire ring.

"Why do you think Luke wants us to spend the night?" Sarah asked me.

I didn't have to wonder about it. "He wants us to make memories."

I smiled to myself remembering how Luke always seemed to over-enjoy things. Growing up with him, he always had to announce that things were fun. He always had to bullet point the good things about an activity. It was like a compulsion. Like he couldn't just have a good time unless he said it was a good time. It made me laugh a little as I realized just how much this quirk had irritated me, as if I had some sort of pent-up rage over something as ridiculous as how someone enjoys things. And yet, I knew I would miss it. I would miss being mad at Luke.

"Well, he's certainly succeeding," Sarah declared in an odd tone. "Let me just off myself and have my friends go on the best damn camping trip ever," she mimicked.

Sarah's sarcasm made me flinch.

"Please don't say things like that."

Her look showed she was surprised with herself, but she quickly resumed scowling.

"Listen," I commanded her. "Don't spoil this for Owen. He's smiling again. I think this is really helping him."

We both were startled by a crashing behind us. Owen had dropped a log from the enormous pile of wood he was attempting to carry back to camp.

Sarah smiled at him and rolled her eyes before looking back over at me and whispering, "Fine."

She pushed herself up off her rock with the palms of her hands. I followed, as she hurried over to help Owen. We set the sticks and logs next to the rusty ring and Owen started forming a stick tent in its center.

"Oh!" Sarah's surprise made us turn our attention to her. "I saw a fish jump!" she said excitedly, pointing toward the reservoir.

Owen stood up and proudly examined his wooden structure. "Now I'm just missing one ingredient," he stated, scanning our surroundings. "Hold up. I'm going to see if someone will lend me a lighter."

He patted me on the shoulder and dashed out of the camp again. I could hear him talking to a stranger nearby.

I gazed up at the night sky. "I didn't realize you could see this many stars," I said, my voice softened by awe.

Sarah also looked up. "Shooting star!" she said louder than I think she meant to.

"Aw, I missed it," I said, feigning disappointment. Sarah was having fun whether she meant to or not.

"Got one," Owen declared happily, appearing behind us. He knelt down and ignited his stick tent with the borrowed lighter.

I watched the tiny flame start to grow as it

climbed up a stick and quickly consumed a cluster of dead leaves.

"I'll be right back," Owen assured us as he left again to return the lighter.

Sarah put her hands up to the flames.

"I brought Owen's blanket," I said.

When Owen returned, I asked him to open his trunk. I retrieved the blanket and tossed it to Sarah.

"Thanks," she said and wrapped it tightly around herself.

The three of us sat down on the ground in a circle around the now blazing campfire. My friends' faces were only partially illuminated by the fire, and the dancing shadows made their features more prominent. They looked exhausted.

"What a day," I said in a half laugh.

"What a day," Owen repeated, staring into the flames. "Wish we had some marshmallows. I don't think I've ever been this hungry."

"It'll make you appreciate tomorrow's dinner that much more," Sarah teased. She appeared more comfortable in her blanket wrap.

"Luke's notes," Owen stated. "They've all been so short. Wouldn't you think he would have more to say to us? Wouldn't you think there'd be pages and pages for us to read? That he would explain himself more to us? That he would at least apologize for what he did?"

"Sometimes you say more by saying less," Sarah mused.

I thought about this as I watched the dancing flames.

"What are we going to do with $30,000?" Owen asked, laughing in disbelief.

"It feels a little illegal, somehow. Like we're stealing," Sarah said, resituating on the ground.

"Yeah," Owen replied distantly. "I'm starting to wonder…I mean, I don't think student loans are meant to be used like this."

We sat there for some time, taking in the growing warmth of the crackling campfire that fought back against the chill of the night. I stared out over the undisturbed water.

When the fire began to die, Owen stood up and opened the door of his car. I could hear him reclining the seat and pushing things around. I watched as the roof of the convertible retracted.

Without saying anything, Sarah and I kicked dirt onto the embers and walked to the car. Sarah turned around and lifted herself so that she was sitting on the side of the convertible. She let herself fall backward onto the back seat. Owen and I got into the front seats. He had reclined mine slightly and we all stared up at the stars.

There was another shooting star! It left a magnificent, lasting streak across the sky. Owen turned to look at Sarah's reaction and then back at me, gesturing with his thumb toward the back seat. I looked over my shoulder and saw Sarah's sleeping body. She was lying with one arm draped over her stomach, breathing slowly. I glanced at Owen who was smiling as he surveyed the water. He shifted in his seat, leaned back, and closed his eyes. It wasn't long before he was asleep, too.

Sitting there looking out over the black water and the surrounding darkened mountains, I felt the hot streaks of tears running down the sides of my face.

Chapter 4
Anything Helps

I woke up in pain. It felt like I had slept upside down. My neck was tight as I massaged it without relief. Now that it was morning, I took in our surroundings again. It seemed like a different world altogether. I could see the colors of the tents surrounding our camp, and could smell coffee being brewed nearby. The chill morning air was carried by a breeze over the water. I shifted my aching body around and saw that Owen was awake. He blinked over at me as Sarah stirred in the back seat. It was as if we all shared the same internal alarm clock.

I heard a mom's failed attempt to yell in a whisper at her child for speaking so loudly this early. The three of us smiled groggily as we struggled out of our still half-asleep state. Sarah was yawning and Owen was rubbing his eyes. I just kept moving my head around, trying to alleviate the pain in my neck.

Over my shoulder, I could see that the larger sticks from the fire were still smoldering. I opened the passenger door and stepped outside the car to stretch. There were birds on the water compelling me to walk down to the reservoir.

We had stayed the night, I thought, as I walked to the water's edge. That's what Luke wanted and that's what we did. It was as if a list were being checked off inside my head. Now to see what other antics he has in store for us, I thought. I knelt beside the water and placed my hands in it. I wondered how water this cold could still be the kind that moves. Still, with cupped hands I splashed some in my face. I was instantly refreshed and much more awake. I jogged back up to the car where Owen and Sarah were talking.

"You ready to go?" Owen asked.

I surveyed the campground once more.

"Yeah," I replied and got back into the car, returning my seat to its original position.

"Finally, some leg room," Sarah said, playfully kicking the back of my seat.

"Sarah, be careful!" Owen gaped at her in horror. "You'll hurt her," he warned softly, while gently petting his dashboard. "You okay, girl?"

Sarah rolled her eyes and I laughed. Owen started the ignition and backed out onto the circle road.

We left the camp and I was relieved to see the ranger from last night wasn't on duty this morning. Sarah was sitting next to the camo container, and I hung my arm over the side of the car to feel the air. Owen had left the top down and, even though it was cold, the wind felt good in my hair. It wasn't long before we were back on the highway.

"I say we each go home for a little bit," Sarah shouted over the sound of the wind. "I have never needed a shower more. Or to shave my legs for that matter."

I watched Owen wince in exaggerated disgust.

"Sounds like a good idea," he said in a tone that

suggested Sarah's having smooth legs was of top priority.

"Also, how are we going to have a fancy dinner with a homeless man? Won't he get us kicked out?" Sarah asked.

"I can borrow my dad's suit coat," Owen said, letting go of the steering wheel to put air quotes on the word "borrow."

"Or we could buy one," Sarah suggested.

"I'd prefer to save our money," Owen explained, laughing. "Don't worry, it's not like he wears it anymore. He won't even know it's gone."

"That still won't do anything about the hair, or smell," Sarah continued.

"So, we're really going through with this?" I asked, being hit by the reality of it all.

"Don't make me stop the car again," Owen threatened. "If it's in the note, we do it."

"That seems like dangerous thinking," Sarah called from the back. "I mean what if he's a rapist or something?"

"He's not going to be a rapist," I interjected. "Still, we could just go to the restaurant," I suggested, looking back at her and feeling slightly guilty for saying it.

"You don't get the whole point of this, do you?" Owen scolded. "Luke wants us to do something good for someone. He's making his death matter. Like the caption on the photo says: Be Kind."

"How do we know the homeless guy will be up for it?" Sarah asked.

"He's not going to say no to a free meal," Owen replied, concentrating on his driving.

Back in the city, Owen dropped Sarah off at her house and started driving toward mine.

"Can I go to your place?" I asked. "I don't really want to be at my place right now."

"Sure, I think you're ready for college," he replied with a grin.

When we arrived in Owen's dorm he threw me the TV remote. "I'll be back in an hour or so, I'm going to go to my parents' place."

I nodded as he closed the door to the dorm.

I lay down on his futon and pulled my phone out of my pocket. Turning it on, I could see the innumerable missed calls and countless unanswered texts. I turned it back off, rolled over, and turned on the television. I put it on mute and watched the soundless people talking.

The door bursting open woke me, and I sat up just as Owen threw me a breakfast burrito. He always tended to throw things that were within handing distance. I only half caught it as he sat down next to me and stared at the TV screen. Together, we ate the burritos and watched the people on TV, neither one of us bothering to turn the sound on or channel surf for something more interesting.

"I'm going to take a shower," Owen announced, licking the last bits of food off his fingers.

"I need one too," I said. "Do you have any clothes I can change into?"

"Yeah," Owen replied, tossing me a towel. "Follow me. I'll show you where the showers are."

Owen picked up his backpack and I followed him down the halls of the dormitory, reading the various posters that promoted safe sex and warned of the dangers of underage drinking. Maybe Owen would be my roommate next year. Maybe I could enjoy going to school here.

The showers were vacant except for us. Owen dug in his backpack for his scattered toiletries and turned on the water. I stepped into the adjacent shower and dropped my clothes on the floor outside the curtain.

The water was the perfect temperature, and the muscles in my neck responded to the therapeutic spray. As I watched the darkened water at my feet flow to the drain, I realized just how dirty I was. My hands were still stained with dirt from digging the night before, and there were little patches of dried blood on them. It was clear that my body belonged to someone going through something terrible, as though I appeared on the outside how I felt on the inside.

"Incoming!" I heard Owen's voice echo, and I jumped as a bottle of body wash hit the floor beside me.

"Ha, thanks." Picking the bottle up from the tile floor, I squeezed out a handful of gel. I covered myself in the soap before tossing it back over the dividing wall to his shower. I heard Owen turn off the water and I did the same. I dried myself with the soft towel, wrapped it around me, and followed him back to his room.

"This might be a bit big on you, but at least it's dressy," he said, handing me some clothes.

I put them on and studied my reflection in the mirror. They did appear large on me, but it would get me into the restaurant without my having to go home. Owen looked much better in clothes that were obviously meant for him.

"I hope this goes well," I said staring out the window of his dorm.

"Yeah, leave it to Luke to have us perform some crazy stunts for him. I'm sure he's quite proud of his social commentary. 'Hey, Mr. Hobo, try some caviar.'"

Owen's phone began beeping.

"It's a text from Sarah," he announced, looking at the screen and chuckling as he read it to me. "'Dinner at five?'"

"Yeah...I'll...pick...you...up," Owen spoke his text slowly as he keyed his response.

I glanced at his alarm clock and saw it was already past noon. The next few hours passed quickly and it didn't seem long before we each were taking one last look in the mirror and getting back into Owen's car.

I stayed in the car as Owen walked up to Sarah's front door and rang the doorbell. She appeared wearing a silver dress. She walked carefully down the front steps of her house in high heels. Something about her hair and makeup suggested she had spent more than the five minutes Owen and I had in the bathroom getting ready. I watched the two of them walking toward the car together. Sarah waved to me, blushing slightly for some reason. I kept pondering Luke's motivations for all this. It felt like some horrible, bizarre prom where a homeless man is your date.

Owen opened the door for Sarah and she slid into the back seat.

"Wow, you've never done this for me before," she said in a girly squeal. "Thank you."

"You look nice," I said, looking back at her as she sat down.

"Well, it is *Mer d'Émeraude*," she stressed in a failed attempt at a French accent. "And thank you," she added after a moment. "You don't look too bad yourself."

Owen swung around and took his place in the driver's seat.

"To Broadway and 9th," he muttered as he backed out of Sarah's driveway.

"What if no one's there?" Sarah asked.

"Well, it can't be that hard to find a homeless person in Sacramento," Owen replied.

"But what if this intersection matters?" Sarah continued. "I've seen days where there's nobody on that corner."

"Well, was it cold outside?"

"Maybe," she replied.

As I sat there listening to them, it was the first time I actually considered the logic of it. Those people. Those homeless people couldn't even beg for money when conditions forced them to seek refuge – most likely in some illegal place – away from the cold.

"Whatever the case, it's nothing but sunshine today. They should be out. Hopefully not listening to headphones like the last person I saw."

"What's that supposed to mean?"

"It's just that some of those people don't actually seem to be struggling at all. Not really. Not with headphones, anyway."

I was surprised by the shift in Owen's opinion of this charity task since our drive back from the campground.

"But, we're just supposed to go by what the note said, right?" Sarah asked, hinting that she had made the same observation.

"Right," Owen replied simply.

As we neared the intersection, I leaned my head over the door to see past the cars ahead of us as best I could.

Sure enough, there was a man holding a cardboard sign. He was next to a car at the red light, getting change from someone inside the vehicle.

"He's there," I said.

"It's usually hookers that people pick up from street corners," Owen said under his breath.

A blaring, honking sounded behind us and I nearly jumped out of my seat. Owen was driving about two miles an hour and infuriating the drivers behind us. He slowly arrived at the intersection just as the light turned from green to yellow. I panicked a bit when I realized I was the one closest to the homeless man and I would have to come up with something to say.

"Hey, man!" Owen called out to him, before I even had a moment to continue worrying.

The man approached us. He looked exactly as I imagined he would with long, dirty, unkempt hair and matching beard. He studied us with furrowed, bushy gray eyebrows. I imagined the rotting teeth that must hide behind those chapped lips.

"You want us to get you some food?" Owen hollered.

"Sure would appreciate it," the man replied.

"Hop in! Eric, open the door. Sarah, scoot over," Owen commanded in a hurried voice over his shoulder.

To my surprise, the man got into Owen's car with no hesitation. I closed the door just as the light turned green. The man had rested his sign carefully near the curb, and I read its message as we drove away. In large letters was written the phrase: "Anything Helps." I glanced in the rear view mirror at Sarah and the man next to her as we drove along. Never in the history of the world could two people have looked any more different.

"We're feeling extra philanthropic today," Owen declared with a forced chuckle to the man. He was good at winging things. "We thought we'd take you to dinner."

"God bless you kids," the man said, and I watched him wipe a tear from his eye.

"What's your name?" Sarah asked.

"Hector," he replied.

"I'm Sarah," she said kindly, "and that's Owen and Eric," she continued, pointing to each of us.

"We're going to a fancy place," Owen explained, "so I brought a nice coat for you."

"I'd be awfully grateful for anything," Hector replied.

We pulled up past the fountain near the entrance to the restaurant. I gazed up in amazement at the classy exterior. Owen stopped and we all got out.

"That's some ride you've got," Hector stated, studying the swage lines on the side of Owen's convertible. "I drove one myself when I was your age."

A valet appeared as Hector put on the coat. It actually disguised a great deal of his tattered clothing. Owen chatted with the young man as Sarah did a final check of her hair and makeup in the reflection of the car. The valet got into Owen's convertible and drove away. Without thinking about it, we found ourselves forming a tight circle around Hector as we walked toward the restaurant's entrance. Sarah adjusted her boobs and confidently led the way.

The interior was filled with paintings and sculptures all representing France and French culture. There was music playing softly and the maitre d' greeted us with a thick accent.

"Such a beautiful lady," he said to Sarah as we approached.

Sarah giggled in response. "We're here to celebrate our grandfather Hector's 80th birthday," she lied.

The host politely nodded at Hector. It was the perfect lie. Force them to be polite, I thought.

"I've got reservations under Parker," Sarah said.

"Right this way, Ms. Parker," the maitre d' stated, and escorted us to a remote table. The restaurant was dimly lit and I struggled to find my way as my eyes adjusted in the dark. We each took a seat around a candle-lit table as a young man approached and poured four glasses of water.

"Your server will be with you shortly," the man assured us as he bowed and stepped away.

We sat there saying nothing to one another, staring at the flickering candle in the middle of our table. It was Hector who broke the silence.

"80th, huh?" he quizzed, staring directly at Sarah.

She was struck with a panicked look. Owen and I looked at Hector. Then, his face broke out in a warm smile.

"I'll have you know I just turned 57, young lady," he said in a pretend scold.

We all started laughing. Sarah was covering her face in embarrassment.

"I hate to jeopardize my chances of being fed, but I have to ask," Hector began. "What are you kids up to?"

We all stopped laughing.

"We lost someone recently," I explained.

For whatever reason, I felt we should come clean with Hector. I felt he was owed our honesty for being dressed up and brought here half disguised by us. Even though Luke may have meant well, the whole stunt, as Owen had described it, easily could have been taken the wrong way.

"I'm sorry to hear that," Hector responded.

"He was a good guy," Owen said, continuing my explanation. "He was all for making a difference even if just in a small way, and, you know, helping others. He believed in God and loved his little sister."

I smiled at Owen. What a perfect summary of our friend, I thought, contented by his words.

"He wanted us to do this," Owen concluded.

"What was his name?" Hector asked.

"Luke," Sarah said for us.

"To Luke," Hector proclaimed and lifted his glass of water.

We all clinked our water glasses together and drank. Just then a young waitress appeared at our table.

"What's the occasion?" she inquired in an attempt to set up a positive introduction for herself.

In a gleeful voice, as though drunk off the water, Hector announced, "My 80th!" He proceeded to give a quick wink at Sarah.

"Congratulations!" the waitress said. "What can I get started for you?"

Dinner continued in a series of laughs and new dishes. We laughed, and learned that Hector had actually been to France. That he had taken his wife there. We learned that his wife had since passed away, that he had two daughters who lived in Florida, and that he had been sober for thirteen years. I felt my negative expectations and prejudices fall off one by one as I got to know more and more about this man who spoke with surprising eloquence.

We ate food that was almost too good to fathom and made comments about the music. I learned things about Sarah and Owen that I never knew as we shared some of our most embarrassing moments – a conversation inspired by someone accidently knocking over their glass. We ordered dessert when it was offered – even though we each had complained earlier about how full we were – and when it came we all shared.

When the conversation took a serious turn, it was Hector who explained himself without any of us asking. He told us that he had been diagnosed with severe depression in his 30's which he attempted to treat with alcohol. He said his mental illness and substance abuse ruined his marriage and tore his life apart, and that it wasn't long before he was living on the streets.

Before we could even respond to what Hector had confided, the server – as though deliberately trying for worst timing – appeared with the check. Sarah pulled her glittery silver purse from under the table as she reached for the check.

"All I have is hundreds," she stated in such a way I couldn't tell if she was joking.

She set a few of the bills on the table. Owen had

become noticeably still next to me. I was about to ask what was wrong when I noticed he was pointing. All of us noticed, and we turned to look in that direction. I only saw the nearby hallway leading to the washroom lounges.

"Do you need help getting there?" I asked, chuckling in nervous confusion.

"What is it?" Sarah was alarmed now.

"That's his," Owen declared, standing up abruptly.

"What are you talking about?" Sarah asked.

"That painting," Owen explained with widened eyes. "Luke made that!"

I turned again and saw the painting he was referring to hanging on a wall to the left of the hallway. It depicted a ship sailing toward the sunset in sea-green waters. Owen walked over to the painting and we all followed. The four of us stared at it. The scene was incredible, and couldn't believe I hadn't noticed it earlier. With a subtle intensity, Luke had mastered Impressionism. His sturdy tall ship sailed peacefully through an emerald sea toward a liquid sunset. Luke's use of color and cues of movement were to be envied.

"See?" Owen asked us, pointing to the bottom right corner of the painting. Sure enough, there were Luke's initials – a double "L" signed in golden ink in lowercase cursive. And below them were numbers.

Chapter 5
Speaking with the Dead

Sarah pulled out her phone once again and I confirmed the new set of coordinates as she entered them.

"Your friend painted this?" Hector asked, respectfully expressing his appreciation for the work.

"Yeah. We need to go," Owen declared matter-of-factly and we left Mer d'Émeraude in a hurry.

"Where would you like us to take you?" Owen asked.

"Same as where you found me," Hector replied, and a horrible guilt filled my stomach.

We drove back to Broadway and 9th, and Hector got out of the car.

"Thank you again," Hector said, taking off the jacket.

"You can keep it," Owen stated.

"No," Hector declined, pushing it into my hands. "Nobody pays a well-dressed homeless."

I heard Sarah in the back fidgeting.

"Here, take this." She pushed a handful of hundreds into the man's hand. "I'm really glad I got to meet you." Sarah wiped a tear from her eye.

"Likewise," Hector replied, his eyes wide as he watched us drive off.

"How much did you give him?" Owen asked, looking at Sarah in the rear view mirror.

"What was left of the bundle," she responded.

"You gave him $10,000?" Owen shouted in disbelief.

"It's my share!" Sarah shot back in retaliation. "That's why he left us three bundles, you idiot! One for each of us."

I could see the veins in Owen's forehead as he glared at Sarah in the rear view mirror.

"That's a lot of money," Owen stated plainly.

"Yeah, well he needs it more than we do," Sarah said looking away. "And it's not ours; it's Luke's."

"Stop it, you guys!" I yelled. I was surprised when they listened. "Why are you so mad, Owen?"

He was silent for a moment as we drove along.

"I'm sorry. That painting just got to me," he explained, shaking his head. "I watched Luke paint that. It was one of his art assignments. I didn't realize he sold it to that restaurant. I guess it just, I don't know, it caught me off guard."

The ever-intruding voice of Sarah's phone interrupted with a last minute instruction to turn.

"My phone says the location is right here in the city. We're pretty close."

"Why didn't Luke just tell us where to go? Why the scavenger hunt?" Owen turned the car abruptly after processing the phone's command.

"I guess he thought it would be fun," Sarah said with an odd tone. "Whatever this place is, it's just another few miles away."

"This is fun?" Owen scoffed.

The traffic was congested now and we were moving painfully slow.

"I'm not sure what this is," Sarah said, shaking her head a bit and gazing out the side window. "Anyway, it's got to be one of those buildings."

The phone's voice indicated we had arrived at our destination and that it was on our right. Owen stopped the car in traffic. The three of us simultaneously turned our heads to read the sign above the door of the building we had been directed to: City Psychic: Tarot, Astrology, Palmistry.

"You've got to be fucking kidding me," Owen cursed as cars behind us started honking again.

Owen pulled over to the curb directly beside the No Parking sign and we all got out.

"You're going to get a ticket," Sarah warned, pointing to the sign.

"It's my share," Owen echoed sarcastically as he walked straight up to the door of the building.

I noticed the bright red OPEN sign in the window. Owen opened the door and we followed him inside.

A home-like setting greeted us. The couches of the room were piled with so many cushions that sitting on them might actually prove challenging. I was drawn to the numerous bookshelves along the wall. Just as I had seen in bookstores, subject plaques hung above them – *Mystic Healing, Spirituality,* and *Auras.* There were crystals and candles displayed along some of the shelves with small price tags underneath. The room reeked of incense and I could hear a small fountain bubbling.

"Welcome," a woman's voice floated from an adjoining room.

The three of us glanced at one another before walking toward the sound of the voice.

Seated behind a small, round table was an overweight woman shuffling cards. She was wearing a robe and several necklaces and bracelets that were magnified by the crystal ball in front of her. Her perfume overpowered the incense, making it difficult to breathe without choking.

"What brings you in this evening?" the psychic asked.

"You tell…"

I cut Owen off with a well-timed cough before he could finish. Having caught his attention, I discreetly whispered to him, "Be kind." Somehow I knew that if there were something here for us to find, or if this woman knew something, it was best to stay on her good side.

"You tell people their futures?" Sarah covered.

"I tell people what chooses to reveal itself," the woman replied. "My name is Roseanne."

I could feel Owen's frustration radiating from his skin. Sarah introduced us.

"Have a seat," Roseanne instructed.

Sarah took the seat immediately across from the woman. Owen and I grabbed two chairs from along the wall and dragged them to the table.

"I offer a variety of reliable psychic readings to those seeking clarity," Roseanne spoke with an air of mystique as she shuffled the deck of cards. "I am happy to assist you in your journey to understanding and mystical fulfillment."

"Do you know anything about our friend?" Sarah asked. "About our friend Luke?"

Raising an eyebrow, the psychic looked at Sarah as though she had been interrupted. "I also accept cash and all major credit cards," she concluded like an actor breaking character.

Sarah and Owen exchanged knowing glances. Owen's chair legs scraped across the floor as he pushed it back to leave. Without asking, I grabbed Sarah's purse and removed a hundred-dollar bill, setting it on the middle of the table. *Some of this is mine*, I thought, and from the corner of my eye I saw Owen smiling, as if to say "Touché."

"Much appreciated," Roseanne said, nodding at me and stowing the cash. Again shuffling her set of tarot cards, she resumed character. "Which method do you desire?"

"Um, how about your cards?" I replied.

"An excellent choice. Shuffle the deck, until you feel ready." She passed me the worn-looking deck.

I shuffled them slightly and handed them back to her.

"Very good," Roseanne replied, placing one of the cards face-up on the table.

Sarah covered her mouth with her hand and Owen stared, gaping in disbelief. Immediately, I concluded that this was some elaborate prank, some horrible sense of dark humor as the horse-mounted skeleton of the Death card appeared before us.

"It is quite clear simply from your reactions to conclude that you have suffered a loss recently," the psychic stated.

"If you know something you need to tell us," Owen threatened before I could even attempt to censor him. I looked to the psychic worriedly.

"I only know what the cards reveal," she responded, unfazed by his anger.

"Did our friend talk to you?" Sarah asked with a distraught voice. "Did Luke come to you?"

The psychic studied Sarah. "I'm afraid I'm not sure what you mean."

"Our friend committed suicide," I explained to her.

"Oh, dear," the medium said, raising that eyebrow again. "I'm truly sorry to hear. You three probably have a lot of questions. Fortunately, necromancy is a service I offer."

I studied the woman in disbelief. What had Luke arranged with her? And why?

"Shall we continue?" she asked.

"No," I replied simply, standing up. Sarah and Owen stared up at me. "Let's go."

As we left her parlor, Roseanne called out from behind us.

"Grief will send you on quite a journey. Your hearts will know pain, yet you will learn to love and smile in new ways." As we continued leaving she added, "Sometimes when we lose someone, it helps to visit the place where they departed this world."

The three of us filed out of City Psychic and

back into Owen's car. I noticed that there was no ticket on his windshield as we all took our seats. Owen pulled back into traffic.

"What the hell was that about?" Owen yelled as he drove. "Do you think Luke arranged that with her? We should tell the police. She has to have done something illegal. Can you be an accessory to suicide?"

"Maybe she didn't know he was going to kill himself," Sarah offered from the back. "I mean, she seemed surprised when we told her what he did."

"What about the Death card? You think that was coincidence?" Owen challenged.

"I helped shuffle the cards, Owen," I reminded him.

"Yeah, well, that deck was probably nothing but Death cards."

"But she asked if we wanted to continue," Sarah stated. "We would have asked about him regardless."

No one responded. Sarah stared out the window. "It's just that, I feel like we're missing something from this. Otherwise, Luke would have had that painting in the restaurant send us directly to his house."

"You think there's something in his room?" I asked.

"I'm not sure," Sarah said. "Probably."

"I can't believe how those people take advantage of others so shamelessly," Owen vented, gripping the steering wheel hard.

"Maybe she thinks she's actually helping people," Sarah replied. "That she's actually gifted."

"Yeah, she's gifted at reading people, and that's it."

Nobody said anything more as we drove to Luke's house.

My bike still lay against the garage as we arrived. The sight of it aroused unwanted memories of first finding out about Luke.

"What are we going to say to his parents?" Sarah asked. "Do you think...do you think we should tell them?"

"No," Owen and I answered in chorus.

"It's getting pretty late," Sarah commented.

"We'll just say we're checking in. I can make this work," Owen assured us.

I began to realize how good at lying the three of us were becoming.

"Shouldn't we change clothes?" I asked, even though the thought of going home now was still troubling.

"No," Owen said as he walked straight toward the front door and rang the doorbell.

We heard footsteps, and then Mrs. Leary appeared at the door. Opening it, she waved us in. I was expecting her to break down at the sight of us, but she remained composed. We all stood there in silence for a moment. Owen studied the floor as he began speaking.

"We thought we owed it to you to pay our

respects," Owen stated. "And to apologize for how we acted when we found out."

Mrs. Leary gave Owen a tight squeeze, standing on her tiptoes to hug him. Wiping a tear from her eye, she turned to Sarah. "You're stunning, darling," she complimented as she examined Sarah's dress and hugged her.

Sarah was wiping her eyes as well. Then, Mrs. Leary turned to me.

"Oh, Eric," she said with a voice full of emotion as she hugged me. I felt a pain in my heart as I hugged her back. "Your mother's worried sick," she said, still squeezing me. "I told her you were safe and with your friends." Then, she looked right at me. Holding onto my wrists gently, she whispered, "Don't shut people out, Eric."

I nodded at her and she let go of my arms.

Despite this show of emotion, Mrs. Leary managed to hold herself together. I was relieved that she hadn't been permanently damaged.

"The funeral will be Friday," she informed us relatively calmly, and the three of us nodded.

"Mrs. Leary," Owen began, "we were wondering if we could visit Luke's room one last time. Just to, you know," he struggled, "say goodbye."

Mrs. Leary nodded her head as her eyes glazed with tears.

"Thank you," Sarah said softly, squeezing Mrs. Leary's hand with more gratitude than sympathy.

Together, we walked slowly up the stairs. Sarah paused halfway up.

"You can do this," I encouraged her, wrapping my arm around her waist for support. Sarah nodded and we continued to the second floor.

The door to Luke's room was closed. Taking a deep breath, Owen opened it. We stepped in and closed the door behind us.

I was stunned by the scene before me. This wasn't at all like I remembered it. Luke's room was completely empty now except for his bed and small side table with a lamp.

"They moved his stuff out?" I asked, incredulous.

"No," Sarah said. "This is how it was when I found him. His stuff is at college," she stated. "Right?"

She turned to Owen for confirmation. Owen didn't respond as he looked around the room. In his silence I remembered Luke's emptied half of their dorm room.

Owen opened the door to Luke's closet. "His guitar's gone," he declared in surprise. Turning around, he continued to survey the empty room. "And so are his speakers." Quietly, half to himself, he stated, "He sold it all. Everything. Even his painting. That's how he got the money."

Sarah and I examined our vacant surroundings, and I felt as empty as the room appeared. Owen walked over to the window and peered out.

"What? Do you think he sold his car, too?" Sarah asked.

"I doubt it," Owen replied. "Nobody in their right mind would buy that piece of junk."

Sarah looked pale. "What are we supposed to find if there's nothing here?"

"There was something in his closet." Owen left the window and crossed the room.

Sarah and I watched as Owen entered the closet and emerged with a large canvas in a wooden frame. Sarah came up next to me and we studied the painting that Owen held from behind. He peered down at it from above as Sarah and I attempted to take in the image that faced us.

The bizarre style looked psychedelic and as if it were created by some mental patient. I examined the deranged painting of an upright guitar that had sprouted skeleton arms and was strumming the intestines out of the naked, dead body draped across it.

The guitar's other skeleton hand was curled around the corpse's neck. Smeared in messy lettering across the bottom was written the caption: Being Played.

Sarah leaned hard against me and put her hand up to her mouth as she moaned.

"There are more," Owen stated flatly, leaning the canvas against Luke's bed and removing another one of equal size from the closet.

"Are you okay with this?" I asked Sarah. She wiped her eyes and nodded resolutely.

Owen turned over the next canvas. It took me a moment to take in the psychotic image. It wasn't violent like the first, but was equally strange. I squinted as I studied it. At the front of the image, a figure towered, facing the viewer, although the frame ended where its head would begin. The figure was holding up its hands as though examining them. It had six fingers on each hand. It stood in a library. The blurry people scattered about the room in the distance appeared to be perusing books and studying. It took me a moment to realize that they all had a disturbing number of fingers on their hands. The caption read: One Thumb.

"What the hell is this?" Owen asked, peering over the top of the canvas he was supporting.

Sarah and I could only shake our heads.

Owen leaned the painting against the first. "There's one more," he mumbled. Sarah and I exchanged glances and nodded at Owen. Slowly, he removed the last painting. The final exhibit treated the viewer to a colorful portrayal of a park full of people. They were all dressed in yellow and pink, and the sun was shining brightly above them. The brightness, however, contrasted severely with the black shadows of the people. Their shadows were depicted with claws that were scraping the ground, struggling in various directions in a desperate attempt to crawl away from the humans. Yet, they remained attached at the feet.

Luke's bedroom door opened and I jumped as though I'd been caught doing something terrible.

Luke's father stood in the doorway. I turned around, positioning myself between Mr. Leary and the painting to conceal as much of the image as I could from him.

"Sorry to alarm you," he said as Owen strategically leaned the last painting against the others so that only the back of the wooden frame could be seen.

"We came to pay our respects," Sarah explained.

"I see."

"How are…how are you doing?" Sarah stammered.

"We're doing alright," Mr. Leary replied, nodding with a serious expression.

Nobody said anything.

"Just thought I'd check in to see if you needed anything," he continued.

"No, we're fine. We'll be going soon," Sarah assured.

Mr. Leary nodded and left the room.

Looking at one another, we began to breathe again. My heart was racing.

"You can't possibly think he hasn't seen these already, can you?" Owen asked. "I mean they're the only things left in the room."

"So, is there something in these paintings Luke wanted us to see?" Sarah asked.

"Maybe there's something else in here," Owen suggested. At once, we all were on our hands and knees in different areas of the room. I peered back into the closet and confirmed that it was now completely empty, as Sarah searched through the side table.

"I found something," Owen said in a distant voice.

Sarah and I scanned the room, but Owen had disappeared. I heard struggling noises and the bed jostled. Owen crawled out from underneath. He was holding a leather-bound journal. Sarah ran up to him excitedly as he stood up.

Owen opened the journal and an envelope fell from between its pages to the floor. Sarah retrieved it. Owen studied a page in the journal, then glanced at the envelope, before returning his gaze to the journal. Puzzled, he inquired, "What does *Pentimento* mean?"

He held Luke's notebook open to us. Written in capital letters across the first page was the word "PENTIMENTO," and the sentence, "You will be shown the way."

"I'll look it up." Sarah keyed the word into her phone. "It means something like repent," she explained, and read a bit more. "It's when an artist makes a change in their painting, but you can still see what was there before."

At once, we each grabbed one of the paintings and studied it more closely. I had to take in the visceral details of the guitar painting again, as I searched for any signs of a change Luke might have made while painting it. Fortunately, my search was a short one as it wasn't long before I heard Sarah say, "Here!"

She rested the bottom of the park picture on the edge of the side table and turned on the lamp. The light shined partially through the lighter parts of the painting.

"The little girl," Sarah said as she pointed to the depiction of a little girl who was holding a yellow balloon and standing near a peacock at a distant point in the park.

"She's the only one who doesn't have a shadow."

"But she used to," Owen said, pointing to the faded dark splotch on the ground next to the girl. The girl's shadow had since been painted over with light green grass.

I studied the entirety of the picture again, this time noticing the caption at the bottom: The Condemned. But it was the change that most intrigued me.

"There are numbers here," I said, pointing to the tiny print along the edge of the artistic correction.

The numbers were so fine that they were barely legible. Sarah keyed the new sequence into her phone and stared at the screen with a look of discomfort.

"What is it?" I asked her.

"It's five thousand miles away."

Chapter 6
Getting Used To Funerals

Sarah picked up the envelope and opened it carefully. She emptied its contents into her hand, fanning out the three slips of paper that had emerged.

It was unmistakable. They were plane tickets.

"They're to Ireland," Sarah announced, examining them in tired resignation.

"When are they for?" Owen asked, "Maybe we're too late."

"No," she responded. "The flight's not until two days from now."

She handed the tickets to me and I studied them. Written on the tickets were the words "First, go sightseeing." I exhaled in a soft laugh as I tried to process it all. "They're First Class," I chuckled as I examined the ticket that read "Harrison, Eric."

We looked over at Owen who wasn't smiling.

"What is it?" Sarah asked.

"That's Friday."

Sarah and I stared at each other.

"Luke's funeral is Friday," Owen clarified.

"It's alright," I reassured them. "We can just buy our own tickets and go after the funeral. We still have plenty of money."

"I don't know," Owen replied. "It does seem like he has us on some kind of timeline. What if we miss something by going later? I mean, there could be something that's time sensitive. I guess that's one thing he didn't account for when planning all this," Owen remarked. "Forgot about his own funeral."

"No, look!" Sarah grabbed the tickets out of my hand. "Right here; the departure's not until 5:00 p.m." She pointed at a column on the ticket. "We just might be able to do both."

I felt a brief sense of relief until Sarah inquired, "Do you guys have passports?"

Owen nodded. Her question bothered me and I couldn't quite put my finger on why. I nodded at her, too, as I did already have a passport. That wasn't what bothered me.

"What about you?" Owen asked her.

"Yeah," Sarah answered, distractedly. "Luke kept pushing me to get one in anticipation of traveling to celebrate our first year of being together, so I did. But we broke up before we made it to a year."

Then I realized why her question had bothered me. It was because Luke had asked me that same question more than a year ago.

A nagging curiosity returned to me.

"Is there anything else in that notebook?" I asked.

Owen picked up the small, leather-bound book and started paging through. "Some weird stuff," he began. "'I bleed paint,' 'Hell's really red,'" he continued, "'Too busy tying strings to shadow puppets.'" He lowered his brow as he finished, still scanning down the page. "These just look like crazy scribbles," he muttered as he flipped to another page. "Hey!"

He held out something to Sarah as we stepped closer to him. Over her shoulder, I saw what she was now holding. It was a second picture – this one of Sarah and Luke. They were kissing in the back seat of a car. At the bottom of the photo was the caption: Be Adventurous.

Owen and I stared at Sarah who was scowling. She looked up at us, then smiled. "I hate this picture," she explained, "and Luke knew it."

We couldn't help but laugh. "But I suppose I can't get rid of it now," she shrugged, and placed it in her purse, along with the tickets and her phone. "Oh, no!" she said, pulling the phone back out and holding it up to us. "It's past midnight! I didn't realize it was so late. We've been here too long. We need to leave."

Owen untucked the back of his dress shirt and slid the journal halfway down the back of his pants before tucking his shirt back in. Sarah and I put the room back exactly how it was when we arrived, and closed the door behind us.

Owen walked stiffly down the stairs as we followed quietly in case Luke's parents had gone to sleep. At the base of the stairs we saw that Luke's parents were still awake and sitting next to each other on the couch. They had an open photo album on the coffee table in front of them. They smiled tiredly up at us.

"I'm so sorry. We didn't realize the time," Sarah apologized.

"It's fine," Mrs. Leary responded. "We wanted you to take whatever time you needed."

Sarah lingered, looking down at the photo album. I could see a picture of Luke with a bald Madeline. He was wearing a gold ribbon on his shirt. Both he and his sister were smiling so big. Smiling like they didn't have a care in the world.

"No one should have to go through what you have been through," Sarah whispered consolingly to Luke's parents.

Luke's father wiped a tear from his eye. "We'll see you Friday," he managed, clearing his throat.

Leaving the Leary's house, I noticed how surprisingly warm it was despite the late hour. Summer really had started even if we weren't ready for it.

"Should we call it a night?" Owen asked and Sarah nodded.

"I'm ready to go home and sleep in my own bed."

Owen and I got into his car.

"I'm going to walk," Sarah said from outside the car, taking off her high heels.

"Are you sure?" Owen asked.

"Yeah," Sarah replied. "I'm only a few blocks away."

Owen nodded. I could sense she would be stubborn if we fought her on it. We maneuvered back onto the road.

"You should go home, Eric," Owen said to me

as he stopped at the stop sign he had blown through just a couple of days ago.

"Yeah," I replied reluctantly. I didn't want to deal with my parents now, but I knew I couldn't put it off forever.

After Owen had dropped me off at my front door, I hesitated. My parents would probably be asleep. Or they would be awake and yelling at me for ignoring them. I unlocked the door quietly and stepped in. I found my mom and dad awake. They stood up and we all just stared at each other before my mom came up and hugged me.

"I kept a dinner in the fridge for you," she stated. "You do whatever you need to do."

It was the best thing she could have said and I felt like I might break down, but I held it together. My dad patted me on the shoulder. "Glad you're safe."

I was oddly amused when I realized there was going to be no confrontation. It made me smile a little, too, that I wasn't the slightest bit hungry. How can so much happen in such a short amount of time, I wondered.

I thanked my parents, went to my room, and shut the door. My phone screen lit up with a text from Sarah. "Pack light. We won't be there for long." Lying on my bed, I closed my eyes and imagined Ireland as I fell asleep.

I joined my parents early at the table for breakfast when I woke up. My mom poured coffee into my dad's cup as he read the newspaper. The newspaper made my mind conjure thoughts of Luke's obituary. It seemed everything served as an upsetting reminder of his death. And yet, my father turned the page and birds chirped outside. The world doesn't slow down for long.

"How are you feeling?" my mom asked as I sat down.

"I'm alright," I half lied. "The funeral's on Friday."

My mother nodded.

"Being with Owen and Sarah is really helping. I think I'm going to be Owen's roommate next year."

"That would be wonderful." My mom smiled at me.

I spent the day going over in my head all of the events of the past 48 hours. My parents didn't pry, which I appreciated. They kept to themselves, and it was almost as if nothing had happened. I ate meals with them, but otherwise stayed in my room. I was packing for Friday – which was taking forever to get here.

I didn't see or hear any more from Owen or Sarah until the funeral. When we did finally see each other again, it was in the church parking lot. The first thing we did was throw our backpacks into Owen's trunk.

Entering the church, I was surprised by how many people were attending. Everyone was hugging and chatting in the foyer. I watched some of them talking to the pastor. Seeing all these people, I imagined each of them receiving the news of Luke's death. I pictured them traveling here. And the whole time I tried to fight a thought I didn't want to claim ownership of. An intrusive thought that I wished my mind weren't responsible for generating. Yet, as I studied Luke's parents who were well-dressed and nodding as they spoke to another family with young children, I kept thinking that the Learys must be getting pretty used to funerals.

We progressed to the sanctuary. Owen, Sarah, and I sat in a back pew next to each other.

The funeral was awful. It was as if none of these people knew Luke at all. They praised him as though he were flawless, which I knew even Luke would be upset by. They spoke about the services he provided to the church, as his images of guts and shadows flashed through my mind. They focused on him being with Madeline now, rather than how he cared for her and looked after her while they were both alive – or how a part of him died when she did. They talked about the grace and forgiveness of God, but they didn't talk about treating mental illness.

We sang a hymn and I imagined him sitting next to me. I imagined him commenting on the funeral. I imagined the jokes he would be making. It was so easy to picture him seated next to me, I couldn't *not* picture it. In a way he was being kept alive by this insane suicide treasure hunt he had devised. And it was nice that he was still here in that way. He didn't have to be gone, I thought. Not yet.

When the service was over, we knew it was time. Sarah, Owen, and I said rushed goodbyes, passing off our haste as being due to overwhelming emotions.

"I told my parents I was going to be staying with you at college a lot this summer," I said to Owen, hurriedly getting into his car and pulling the door closed.

"Mine think I'm going to spend the time visiting my sister in Washington," Sarah explained from the back. "She said she'd cover for me if I didn't tell them where *she* was spending the summer."

We started laughing as we drove toward the Sacramento airport. I studied Sarah's phone that, once again, had found its way onto the divider between the front seats. The airport was more than an hour's drive from the church.

"Do you think we'll make it in time?" I worried, studying our glittery-pink navigator.

"Not if traffic stays like this," Owen responded, just as we approached a deadlocked highway.

The pace was painstakingly slow as we crept along.

"We cannot miss this flight," Sarah said to the window.

"We won't," Owen reassured, pointing ahead of us.

Slowly, we passed two stopped cop cars with flashing lights, an ambulance, and what was left of a totaled car. I assessed the damage. There was no way anyone could have survived that accident, I thought, as traffic immediately got back up to speed.

As we drove toward the airport, I kept thinking

about that wreck. Whoever undoubtedly died in that car accident didn't get to say goodbye. They didn't get to give their friends photographs or leave them notes. They didn't get to make them make memories. They were just dead. In an instant. Leaving those behind them to grieve. And even though it seemed wrong, that final thought caused some small part of me to envy Luke. The problems of the world weren't his problems any longer. He wouldn't have to be the one to miss us when *we* died.

When we arrived at the airport, Owen pulled into a long-term parking structure. Grabbing our luggage from Owen's trunk, we hurried into the airport with twenty minutes remaining until our flight. We raced past people and waited fearfully at the check-in. I was convinced our rushing was all in vain when we reached security. After Owen and I were through, Sarah kept activating the detector. She continued to set off the alarm as security found more and more items on her person that were setting it off. Owen and I stared at her in disbelief.

"Are you serious?" Owen asked her condemningly.

"I'm sorry," Sarah mouthed to us, as she was being patted down by the noticeably suspicious airport security agent.

Finally clearing security, Sarah jogged up to us. Together, we ran to our gate. Passengers were boarding as we arrived.

"Thank God," Owen said as we joined the line

of passengers filing past the attendant on their way to the boarding bridge.

The attendant scanned our tickets and handed them back to us, expressionless. I looked at her not looking at us for a moment before boarding the plane.

Chapter 7
The Greatest Names for a Band

Upon boarding the plane, we were immediately directed to First Class seating.

"Looks like he gave me the window seat," Sarah stated less-than-enthusiastically as she checked the seat number against her ticket and slid in. Owen slid in next to her. My seat was on the other side of the aisle.

The seats were wide and comfortable with thick armrests between them. There were high-definition television screens built into the backs of the seats in front of us.

"You alright?" I heard Owen ask.

Hearing this, I turned to them and was alarmed by Sarah's paleness.

"I'm okay," she answered. "I've just never flown before. I'm a little nervous."

"Come on," Owen remarked, reaching over the armrest and squeezing her knee. "Be adventurous," he teased.

Sarah managed a weak smile and nodded quite seriously in response.

I felt exhilarated as the plane took off. I wanted to leave this place; I wanted to fly away. And we actually were! I relaxed in my seat as we broke through the clouds. *Thank you, Luke,* I thought as we ascended, and I gazed out the window over the empty seat next to me at the pink sheet of clouds that now divided us from the world below.

When we were free to remove our seatbelts, I retrieved Owen's backpack from the overhead compartment, and took out Luke's journal. Owen was playing with the screen in front of his seat and Sarah was gazing out her window. Her color had returned, but her seatbelt remained fastened as she gripped her armrests tightly.

I opened Luke's journal and scanned over the odd scribblings that Owen had read to us earlier in Luke's bedroom. I turned the page. "Our lives are impossible," "What starts a beating heart?" Further down the page my eyes struggled to discern an almost illegible sentence: "There is such a thing as knowing too much."

What did all of this mean? It was like peering into Luke's mind, and I wondered if that was why he left all this for us to find. That perhaps it was his way of explaining himself to us.

I turned to another page and was surprised to find a roughly sketched cartoon. Within the cartoon square was depicted a stickman with marker blood shooting out in exaggerated spurts from his body. Around him, doctors were running away. His agonized word bubble screamed, "Why did I eat so many apples?"

"Look at this," I said to my friends as I passed them the journal.

Owen read the comic and laughed before

handing it to Sarah. She studied it for a while and turned the page.

"There's a lot of stuff in here," she observed. "Here's a list," she continued, "'Greatest Names for a Band.'"

"Number one," she announced, "'Chocolate Coffins.'" She read this in a half-declarative, half-skeptical tone. She raised her eyes to us. Owen was smilingly, clearly amused. Sarah resumed reading.

"'Frozen Refrigerators,'" she laughed at the absurdity of the words as she spoke them. She scanned further down the page. "What's 'DSLV'?"

"Dialogue, Sex, Language, and Violence," Owen replied. "Like the TV ratings."

I laughed at that one. Owen and Sarah smiled at my laughter.

"'Weigh Yourself Naked,'" Sarah said, and apparently burdened by its ridiculousness, she passed the journal back to Owen with a limp hand.

Owen, smiling, turned to a new page. In a suddenly serious voice he read, "'Please, God, give us a cure for cancer.'"

Slight turbulence and the bing of the seatbelt icon's appearance brought us back to reality. I heard Owen reassuring Sarah.

"I still can't believe he's dead," Sarah muttered loosely, probably in an attempt to distract herself. "I wonder if maybe Luke was schizophrenic or something."

I could hear a baby crying behind the privacy curtain that divided the First Class section from

Coach. Even I began to take note of the growing rumble of the plane.

"He did take a lot of medication," Owen said. "But I never thought I should ask what for."

"Did you know that there are guidelines about how the news reports suicides?" Sarah asked us. "Sometimes when a person kills themselves, a bunch more people do the same thing. There's even a name for it. They're called 'suicide clusters.' Isn't that horrible?"

As I considered her comments, I first thought that maybe this happened because of all the people saddened by their loss. But if how the suicide was reported contributed to the rise in suicides, I wondered if maybe it was because the reporting made suicide seem like an inviting option. Or maybe a way to get attention. Can someone enjoy the promised attention of suicide before they actually die? Did Luke?

"Just promise me that you guys will talk to me first," Sarah said, white knuckling her armrest. "Or to *someone*, if you start feeling sad."

"Same goes for you," I replied.

"I also heard once that if people aren't given the opportunity to kill themselves, like if they go to jump off a bridge but barricades have been put up or something, it can save their life. It's called 'means restriction.' Isn't that fascinating?" Sarah asked. "That such a huge thing can be prevented if a person is just made to think clearly for a moment?"

Sarah paused for a few seconds as if thinking about her own words.

"So, what – were we just supposed to tell Luke he could never wear a belt?" Owen challenged.

Sarah glared at him. "How can you even say something like that?"

The unwelcome image of Luke hanging was forced back into my mind. Had he given any thought to his body being discovered? With all of his other planning, why was there no evidence of forethought in the actual method he chose?

"I'm just saying that it's silly to think it's our fault," Owen replied. "If I could have done something, I would have. I never saw this coming."

"That's not at all what I'm suggesting." Sarah's expression softened. "I didn't mean for you to take that personally. I just meant that maybe if he had gotten some therapy he'd still be here."

Owen leaned back in his seat. "Counseling wouldn't have helped. It's just a bunch of well-dressed, pseudo professionals nodding along to what you say."

Sarah shot Owen a hateful glare. "No it isn't!" she hissed and turned her back to him, looking out her window with her arms crossed.

"He would have hated counseling," Owen spoke to Sarah's back. "He probably would have called them out on all their bullshit and painted pictures of them sitting on thrones of money."

"Shut UP!" Sarah yelled, glaring back at Owen.

I noticed other passengers looking over at us.

"Be quiet," I commanded my friends in a harsh whisper.

At this, Sarah lowered her head and leaned in closer to us. "I had a friend who used to hurt herself," she continued, more quietly. "She was really depressed. She said that living with depression was like living on fire and constantly wanting to put it out, but not being able to. I remember her telling me that when you're that depressed everything around you, every conversation you overhear, makes you sorry to be a part of this world. Like you can see through people. Like everything's fake; everything's scripted."

Sarah took a deep breath and continued softly. "She used to cut herself because she said it made everything 'right.' She said she craved it, and that it was better than *sex*." Sarah leaned in even closer to Owen, invading his personal space. Her eyes locked on his. "She probably would have killed herself if she hadn't gotten treatment. Now she's going to school to become a therapist. An *art* therapist," she emphasized, before returning to her window-facing position.

Owen looked at me and raised his eyebrows.

Still staring out the window, Sarah continued. "She said something else that stuck with me. She said that there are some things that can't easily be described. But there are attempts to describe them. And that art is both."

Sarah paused, and turned to Owen. "My friend probably would have loved Luke's art. And she'll probably be in too much debt from school to be sitting on any 'throne of cash,'" Sarah mimicked Owen's words sarcastically. "She just wants to help people. Like she was helped."

Owen stared at her, opening his mouth slightly as though struggling for a reply.

"Stop arguing, you guys," I commanded, wanting to put an end to their conversation. "This isn't what Luke wanted this trip to be about. Look around us. We're in freaking First Class on our way to Europe!" I hoped to bring them back to the excitement we were feeling before.

"Sorry," Sarah apologized.

"Me, too," Owen eventually concluded, replacing whatever words were in his mouth.

The plane steadied as though its problem with turbulence were settled along with my friends' argument. The flight, however, proceeded to drone on for hours. We ate the meals that were served to us, and each fell asleep at one point.

"We're almost there," Owen whispered to me as he headed down the aisle to the lavatory. I glanced over at Sarah who was rubbing her eyes and smiling weakly.

Owen was hurried back to his seat by a stewardess. The pilot announced our beginning descent, and soon we were preparing to land. I heard Sarah gasp in amazement, and she pointed out her window. I looked out my window again, this time observing the Emerald Isle below.

Upon landing, we waited to be released from

the plane and then hurried through the airport. Owen stopped us at a currency exchange kiosk and Sarah handed him some of our bills. When we stepped outside the airport, we breathed in the cool afternoon air.

"Well, apparently we're supposed to go 'sightseeing' before we look for the coordinates," Sarah reminded us.

"Why don't we find where we'll be staying first?" Owen suggested, hailing a taxi. "Can you take us to a youth hostel nearby?" Owen asked the cab driver as we climbed in. The man nodded.

I stared out the window of the cab as I heard Owen chatting with the driver. I watched the many people on the streets, and read the names on the street signs. Hardly outside the airport, this place already felt entirely different from California. When had Luke come here, I wondered. Had he made such a long trip alone while planning all of this? How did we not know? I guess there was a lot we didn't know about Luke. And there was a lot we were finding out.

The taxi driver pulled up alongside a small building. Murphy's Hostel, according to the sign on the front.

"Let's pay the man," I heard Owen's voice call cheerfully from the front of the car as he passed over a handful of our new colorful euros. The driver nodded with a smile. I watched as he drove away, past a magnificent-looking cathedral that we would definitely have to explore when sightseeing.

We checked into the hostel and tossed our

backpacks on the floor. Each of us collapsed on our beds and sprawled out, as though trying to take up as much space as possible.

"Where do you want to go first?" Sarah asked, rolling over on her side and looking at us.

"There was a cathedral just up the road," I suggested.

"Cool," Sarah replied, hopping up from her bed.

Back out on the street, we walked toward the cathedral. From the little shops along the way, I could hear passersby speaking in thick Irish accents.

The cathedral loomed over us as we approached. Appreciating the architectural features and complicated design, we entered.

The sanctuary was quiet except for the pleasant sound of a choir singing in a distant loft. Owen peered over curiously at the confessional booths on one side of the vast sanctuary. Sarah and I wandered behind the pews to get a better view of some of the enormous stained-glass windows on the other side. I stood next to Sarah and we stared upwards studying the depictions in the glass.

"This is breathtaking," Sarah exhaled. She smiled over at me and looked up again.

"Yeah, it is and so is the singing," I said to her.

We stood there for some time observing the holy art and listening to the choir before the calm surroundings were disrupted by a piercing shriek. Startled, Sarah and I jumped. Before we could even turn around to determine the source of the screaming, I felt something pulling me roughly by my wrist out of the sanctuary. Our surroundings were a blur, but my mind eventually registered that Owen was dragging Sarah and me behind him while booking it toward the outer doors of the church. Outside, we struggled to keep up with Owen's pace and not trip over ourselves as he ran, full speed, pulling us down the street behind him.

"What are you doing?" Sarah yelled.

Owen rounded a corner and whipped us around it with him. We were flung against the side of a building. Bent over, we gasped for air.

"What the hell are you doing?" Sarah repeated, rubbing her wrist.

"I just punched a nun," Owen said with a shocked expression on his face.

"What?" Sarah asked, confused.

Owen held his stomach as he continued breathing rapidly. As he attempted to breathe, he attempted to explain.

"I was by the confessionals. I started talking with this nun lady. I told her about Luke – that he committed suicide." Owen wiped the sweat from his forehead. "And she said that he was in hell," Owen stated. "She just said it in this way…I don't know how to describe it. Like she pitied me, but not really. Like she was warning me or something. And I just lost it. I swear my hand moved itself!"

"Did she…" Sarah struggled to ask, "did she…survive?"

Something about the way Sarah asked her question and the ridiculousness of the entire situation made me start laughing. I couldn't stop. I laughed this hysterical, gut-grabbing, and evidently contagious laugh – with Sarah and Owen joining in. No longer able to stand, we slid to a sitting position with our backs against the building, and laughed uncontrollably.

"I didn't know I could run that fast!" Owen managed, wiping tears out of his eyes.

"Neither did I!" Sarah added, taking our laughter to new heights.

Finally, our laughter died down even though we were still holding our stomachs.

"Did anyone see you punch her?" Sarah asked.

"Just her. Actually, I don't even think she saw it coming," Owen chuckled. "No. Nobody saw it and I was running before she even had a chance to start yelling."

"I say that's enough 'sightseeing' for us," Sarah offered.

"Yeah," Owen replied. "Let's see where this thing is."

Sarah pulled out her phone and studied it as she walked. Owen and I followed her. Fortunately, the coordinates were leading us away from the church.

"It's not too far," Sarah called back to us. "Not anymore, anyway," she added, glancing over her shoulder at us and smiling.

I smiled, too, as I considered just how far we now were from Luke's bedroom. And what an experience! Being so far from home. Being surrounded by such unique culture. Getting to see another part of the world we live in. Absorbing everything with all my senses – observing, experiencing, learning – I felt like I was meant to be here.

"It's just up ahead," Sarah yelled in excitement, and began running. We chased her a few blocks, before coming to a sudden stop.

Music and laughter could be heard coming from inside O'Donnell's Pub.

Chapter 8
Sláinte

We exchanged what-has-Luke-done-now glances as we approached the pub's entrance. The patrons stared at us as we entered. The men seated about turned their attention back to the drinks on their tables as soon as the door closed behind us, blocking out the sunlight and restoring the familiar dark.

The bartender nodded at us politely. I took notice of a clock, and found I'd been disoriented from the change in time. It was three in the afternoon.

"Drinking age is eighteen here," Owen commented, walking up to the bar.

I hadn't even thought of that. Sarah smiled at me as she slipped her phone into her pocket and caught up with Owen. Supposing it would appear odd if we didn't act as patrons, I joined them.

"What do you want?" Owen asked Sarah.

Sarah grinned thoughtfully with a finger on her lip before pointing at a sign advertising Irish whiskey.

"Straight whiskey?" Owen raised a brow. "Damn. What about you, lightweight?"

I shrugged my shoulders and nodded.

"Three whiskeys," Owen ordered.

The bartender nodded and set three glasses on the bar in front of us. Retrieving the appropriate bottle, he expertly filled each glass to the perfect level.

"Cheers," he said to us as Owen slid him one of our purple European banknotes.

"I assume you want me to keep this open?" The bartender joked in a thick accent, impressed by the denomination of the bill.

"Sure," Sarah replied chuckling.

We took our drinks to a table across the room and sat down.

"To Luke," I said and lifted my glass.

"And Hector," Owen replied smiling.

"And Hector," Sarah and I chorused.

Our glasses clinked loudly with the sincerity of our toast.

I wondered how Hector was doing as I took my first sip. I wondered how far $10,000 could get a homeless man. My thoughts were interrupted by the sting of the whiskey. Owen winced as he swallowed, too.

"Smooth," Sarah declared holding up her glass and examining the malt color appreciatively.

We all laughed.

"Alright," Sarah said, getting serious as she moved her head in closer to us. "Let's find this thing. And let's try not to draw too much attention to ourselves."

Sarah removed her phone and stood up. Owen and I remained seated and watched Sarah's failed attempt at being inconspicuous as she struggled to navigate through the room. She kept glancing at her phone and bumping into chairs – many of them occupied – as she awkwardly tried to follow the coordinates. The task proved a difficult sport to play indoors. Owen laughed and took another drink. I tried my drink again, finding it more tolerable now that I had some idea of what to expect.

Sarah had paused, and completely turned around in place, before marching in the opposite direction. It was as if she had given up trying to be discreet altogether, as she walked in a diagonal line through the pub and disappeared down a hall.

Owen continued drinking, with Sarah seeming to provide all the amusement he needed. I craned my neck trying to see where she had gone. Appearing again, she hurried back to our table. Some of the barflies were ogling her over the brims of their beer glasses.

"Well, I need you guys' help," she said in an annoyed whisper. "It's in the little boys' room."

Owen nearly spewed his drink.

"Well, that's convenient," he replied. "I need to take a piss anyway."

Owen stood up and I followed him into the bathroom. I examined the walls of the small room, while Owen made use of the urinal. My eyes caught the colorful walls of the bathroom's single stall. I stepped inside. All of the walls were covered in graffiti – so much so that newer additions layered the older. Some creations were profane and some showed surprising talent. There were statements praising Ireland, many more were random expletives. My eyes scanned over several crude phallic drawings and jokes about women as I continued searching.

I was certain that if Luke were to have left us a message, this was the place it would be. The only place it could be hidden in plain sight. I looked to the lower corners of the stall. Almost hidden by the base of the toilet near the floor I saw it – Luke's gold initials.

"I found something!" I hollered to Owen who quickly appeared behind me. I got down on my knees and wedged myself between the toilet and the wall to get a closer view. I read what was written next to the initials.

Have a few here on me and please keep the commitment I made.

Ending the statement was a drawing of a golden paw print.

I squeezed myself out of my tight quarters and stood up at once. "Rowdy," I said to Owen. "He wants us to take care of his dog."

I sidled around Owen so that he could get a clearer view. He leaned down and read the message.

"Let's tell Sarah!" Owen said excitedly, as we tried to exit the cramped stall.

We encountered the strange look of a man standing at the urinal as Owen and I stumbled out of the stall together.

Returning to our table, we found it to be unoccupied. Sarah was gone and her now empty glass served as the only evidence she'd ever been there.

"There she is," Owen stated, pointing to the bar.

Sarah had taken a seat there and we sat down on the stools on either side of her. The bartender nodded at us again.

"This is Patrick," Sarah introduced us, giggling. "I like your ring," she said dreamily, as Patrick handed her another glass of whiskey. Owen peered over his shoulder at our half-full glasses sitting next to Sarah's empty one on the table. He returned his focus to Sarah with a what-the-hell expression.

"Thanks," Patrick replied as he explained his Claddagh ring to her. I examined the crowned heart and hands on the sterling ring around his finger. "And when you wear it like this," he continued, "it means your heart's still unclaimed."

"Oh, that's sweet," Sarah giggled as she ran her fingertips down Patrick's hand.

Owen and I exchanged glances of horror.

"Well, we're back from the bathroom," Owen announced rather loudly.

Sarah stared blankly at him.

"How about two more," Owen requested, despite our unemptied glasses on the table behind us.

Patrick quickly poured Owen and me another round.

"Well, what did you find?" Sarah asked us loudly.

Owen glanced uncomfortably at Patrick.

"It's fine," Sarah continued, still loudly. "I already told him why we're here."

Owen scowled at her, annoyed.

"Well, you told that nun!" Sarah said defensively and Owen blushed.

I kicked Sarah's leg. She looked at me and returned the gesture.

Owen drank deeply from his glass. I took a larger swallow than I meant to, but managed to keep from choking.

"I'm sorry for your loss," Patrick stated.

I studied him, trying to read what kind of a person he was. He seemed sincere as he said this.

"It's truly a terrible thing to have to deal with," Patrick continued when nobody said anything. "But, hey, I mean there must have been a reason he had you come here."

"He wants us to spend some time here," Owen said. "And adopt his dog."

"Rowdy?" Sarah asked staring with wide eyes at Owen.

We nodded and I took another drink.

"Aww!" Sarah squealed. "Rowdy's his little Lab puppy," she explained to Patrick. "He's only a few months old."

"You like dogs?" Patrick inquired, leaning closer to Sarah and giving her his undivided attention.

"I love dogs," Sarah replied softly.

Would Luke want this? I wondered as I watched their exchange. Would Luke want his ex-girlfriend hitting on somebody now? I had to remind myself that he was gone. It still felt like he was right next to us, communicating with us. Like he was still dating Sarah. But he wasn't. And maybe he wouldn't mind their flirting. Maybe he would want whatever made her happy.

"Do you think his parents will be alright with us adopting him?" Sarah asked, taking another sip from her drink.

"I'm not sure," Owen replied. "Seems like kind of an awkward situation."

"That was all that the message said?" Sarah asked. "There weren't any coordinates?"

"No," I answered, and could sense a strange quietness fall over us.

Our silence was interrupted by the scraping of chairs being dragged across the floor. A small group of people had arrived in a corner of the tavern. Patrick greeted them excitedly and stepped out from behind the bar to help them set down the many instruments they were carrying in.

"These are my new American friends," Patrick said to them as he introduced us. "This is Sarah, and er," he hesitated.

"Owen," Owen said flatly.

"I'm Eric," I said to them, smiling in an attempt to be friendly.

The woman nearest me shook my hand.

"This is The Band," Patrick said, introducing the group. "They're here every weekend."

"How's about a drink there, Patrick?" one of the men near the back of the group shouted. Sounds of agreement echoed amongst the five of them.

Patrick hurried back behind the bar.

"What brings you to Ireland?" the woman asked us.

"We lost someone," Sarah explained. "We're sort of scattering ashes."

"Terribly sorry for your loss," the woman said gently. Her accent made her words difficult to understand, as though she weren't even speaking English.

"He wanted us to come here," I explained to her.

"Well, you've come to the right place, dear," the woman reassured. "How's about we play a little song for your friend?"

"That'd be great," I said, smiling.

The Band gratefully accepted their beers from Patrick as they continued setting up their instruments. Other people began to fill the room around us. Patrick was busy serving them. We waited in excitement for some time as the group finished setting up.

The woman spoke gently into the microphone. "We'd like to play a song for you all," she announced to the bar.

Sarah, Owen, and I exchanged amused glances as we drank.

"It's a bit of a sad song," she warned the crowd.

I enjoyed the sound of her voice and her stage presence. How she could so calmly speak to the crowd as though they were old friends.

"It's a song about loss," she continued. "But more importantly, it's a song about new beginnings, new opportunities," she explained with a wink in our direction.

With a nod back to the other band members, the woman started singing and was at once accompanied by her fellow musicians. The customers had stopped ordering drinks and Patrick had sneaked around the bar to take a seat beside us as we watched the performance.

The woman's voice was beyond beautiful. As I listened to her words and looked around the room, the experience was almost spiritual. As though Luke's death were being properly memorialized. I felt the hairs on the back of my neck stand on end with her haunting melody, and it was as though the moment were consecrated somehow. And right now, here in the bar, I felt how I had wanted to feel at the church. Like, finally, Luke was being paid proper tribute. It seemed this pub was somehow serving as a better place than his church for a funeral – attended by strangers and half-sober friends, and led by the angelic singer of a band.

I felt Sarah's gentle hand on my leg, and we looked at each other. We both shed tears as the woman's voice continued to fill our ears with its ethereal beauty. And when she stopped, when it was all over, we wiped our eyes and clapped our hands.

The woman took a small bow. "But we mustn't linger on loss," she persuaded soothingly into the microphone when the applause had finally quieted. "Who amongst us would leave this world with a wish only to be remembered in tears?" Every flourish of her accent seemed to ring her words more true. "Wouldn't we want to be remembered in all the times we shared smiles?"

I heard the loud agreement of some unseen man from the crowd.

"Our next song is about the moments to remember. It's also one that begs a good dance," she added, winking enticingly to the crowd.

There were cheers from the crowd as The Band started up again with a rapid, excited beat and foot-tapping musicians. Owen, Sarah, and I were beaming as we watched a young couple run up to the front of the crowd and start dancing enthusiastically.

Patrick placed new drinks in front of us, and poured one for himself, as well. "Sláinte!" he shouted, raising his glass. The four of us toasted emphatically.

The pub was full now as the band played on. Patrick was joined by other bartenders. I felt a strong, universal sense of belonging filling the room as though all these strangers were our best friends. Everyone laughed and danced and drank.

Eventually, we stumbled out of the pub back into the cool night air. It was drizzling as Sarah, Owen, and I attempted to navigate our way back to the hostel that started with an "M."

I followed crookedly behind my friends as Owen attempted to steady Sarah's walk, even though he was clearly the one leading them off a straight path. We collapsed, once again, onto our beds back at the hostel.

Waking to the sound of Owen dry heaving in

the bathroom, my head had never hurt more. I checked on Sarah who was still asleep. The sounds of Owen vomiting motivated me to wander over to him.

"Fuck you, Luke," Owen said in a half laugh, wiping his mouth and looking over at me with bloodshot eyes.

"You alright?" I asked.

"Never better," Owen replied, standing up and flushing the toilet. He followed me out of the bathroom. Sarah was awake now and sitting up in her bed.

"Morning, guys," she greeted us cheerily.

"How are you not hung over?" Owen groaned.

"Patrick kept pushing water on me," she answered.

Digging around in the pocket of her jeans she eventually extracted a piece of paper with numbers scribbled on it.

"Score!" Sarah stated in a deep, man-voice. "I'll make him wait a few days before I call," she continued, throwing all semblance of femininity to the wind.

Owen made a horrible moaning noise as he ran back to the bathroom.

"Rest up," Sarah called out loudly, her voice returning to its normal tone. "I'll go get some stuff to help you feel better." Grabbing her purse, she headed for the door. "You boys need to learn how to handle your liquor," she scolded, clearly enjoying herself as she left the room.

Chapter 9
Songs for the Road

Owen and I slept through the rest of the day after Sarah returned with medicine.

"Wake up!" Sarah yelled. "Our plane leaves in a few hours."

Thankfully she had been paying attention. I hadn't even thought about our return. It was sad to leave Ireland so soon, but I did feel like we had done what we came to do.

There was a nagging feeling, though, that had nothing to do with our return flight. Besides adopting Luke's dog, our tasks had ended. We didn't have anything else to pursue. There were no more coordinates, no more leads. I felt this was the end of the journey. It was a good grand finale, I considered appreciatively, thinking about the "funeral" at the tavern. It had been a great send-off. But it meant the end.

On the flight home, I could sense Owen and Sarah felt the same way as we hardly spoke. Each of us kept to ourselves. I started thinking about the future. About college. Wondering what I wanted to major in. I thought about turning nineteen. It felt good to think about other things for a change. And I felt guilty for it.

When we returned to the States, we each spent the next few days at our own places. It was probably best to be apart for a while, having been sort of prisoners of each other's company with this obligation to Luke. How many arguments had we had during our adventure?

It wasn't until after I got a text from Owen that the three of us saw each other again. I read the message with a smile: "Want to take the puppy for a W.A.L.K.?"

When the three of us arrived at Luke's house, I wondered how we were going to go about asking his parents for Rowdy. Did I even have the time to take care of a dog right now, I wondered. Did any of us? It was quite the commitment Luke passed off to us, and given the circumstances, it was kind of obligatory.

We knocked on the Leary's door and Mrs. Leary greeted us. The three of us stepped into the living room and glanced over at the small divider to the adjacent room that contained the dog.

"Just wanted to visit," Owen began.

"Can I get you three anything?" Mrs. Leary asked politely.

"No, thanks," Owen replied, peering around the room. "Where's the puppy?"

Mrs. Leary lifted her eyebrows as he asked this. "He's napping in the other room," she replied.

"I wonder," Owen began, "would you mind if we took him for a walk?"

Mrs. Leary studied us with a strange expression, and after a lengthy pause said, "Yes, yes, that would be wonderful. Feel free to spend all the time you want with him." Leading us toward Rowdy's kennel she warned, "He's a bit of a handful. Rick and I have a hard time keeping up with him. He could definitely use the attention."

Mrs. Leary left the room. The three of us stepped over the divider, and I realized the sight of a puppy waking up and recognizing new people in the room is one of the most wonderful moments life has to offer.

Rowdy's tail started wagging at once as the little Golden Lab shot from deep sleep to maximum energy within seconds. He jumped on us, only reaching our knees. He seemed unable to focus his excitement on any one of us as he barked and ran to the next person who happened to catch his attention. The little puppy struggled in a hilarious attempt to keep up with his own excitement. We all giggled and took a seat in a circle around him. Taking this as an invitation, he bounded up to each of us and began hyperactively licking our faces.

"Watch the junk," Owen groaned, lifting the little dog off his lap with one hand and setting him back down in the middle of our circle, only to have him run immediately back to where he'd been.

"Rowdy," Sarah whistled and the dog darted over to her. We started taking turns calling his name until, finally, the little Lab collapsed on Sarah's lap and gave in to being lazily petted. Sarah scratched the puppy behind the ears as he panted. I smiled at his protruding tongue as it drooled onto the carpet.

Sarah's smile shifted peculiarly.

"What is it?" I asked as her expression became increasingly more perplexed.

Holding the little bone-shaped tag on Rowdy's collar between her fingers, she flipped it over so Owen and I could see the series of numbers engraved on it.

038 0 029 123 0 024

We leapt to our feet. Sarah held Rowdy in one arm with his paws resting on her chest. She reached into her pocket with her free hand to retrieve her phone, exhibiting all the juggling skills of a new mom. I took the little puppy from Sarah as she keyed in the new coordinates.

"How's about that walk?" Owen reiterated, jerking his head toward the door.

"Or *drive*," Sarah replied, looking up from her phone.

"Mrs. Leary," Owen called to the other room, still looking at Sarah. "Would you mind if we took Rowdy to a park?"

Mrs. Leary appeared in the entryway. "Like I said, you kids can spend all the time you'd like with him. He's all yours."

"You know," I began, staring down at the little panting dog I was holding. "If he's too much for you, we'd be happy to take him off your hands. I mean, I'm sure my parents would welcome this little guy."

I worried I had done something terrible as Mrs. Leary's eyes filled with tears. She disappeared to another room. I looked at my friends fearfully. Then, Mrs. Leary reappeared holding some papers and a set of keys. Wiping her eyes before she spoke, Luke's mom looked at the three of us.

"It said in the note," she began. "In *our* part of the note," she struggled. "It said he wanted you three to be the ones to take care of Rowdy." At this point, her tears gave way to sobs. "But only if you asked." Attempting to compose herself a bit, she added, "He also wanted you to have his car." She handed Sarah the stack of papers and Owen the set of keys. I studied the adoption forms Sarah was holding. Her hands shook.

"Are you sure?" Owen questioned, examining the keys in his hand.

"It's in Rick's name," Mrs. Leary responded. "He already transferred the title to you. You just need to sign and file it. That old car," she continued, wiping away a tear and laughing a little as she shook her head. "You'd be doing us a favor."

Mrs. Leary led us out to their double-wide garage and opened the overhead door. We stared at the four-wheeled atrocity before us. Not our best inheritance, I thought amused. But it was free. Dents along the side of the rusted brown car did nothing to enhance its appeal. Owen got in the driver's seat and thanked Mrs. Leary through the window.

"Wait, let me grab some of Rowdy's things," Mrs. Leary said.

She returned from the house with the small kennel she had stuffed with Rowdy's toys. Owen got out and opened the trunk. We stared in surprise as we took in the sight before us. The trunk was full of several bags of dog food, a larger kennel, unopened toys, a leash, and a full-sized doggy bed. I looked over at a stunned Mrs. Leary. She was holding her free hand over her mouth, speechless.

"Thanks," I said awkwardly, taking the kennel from her and pushing it in next to the larger one. I feared the sight before us was about to motivate Luke's mom to ask the question we all silently knew she wondered but never voiced. In my head I could so easily hear her asking, "What did those numbers mean?"

Mrs. Leary remained silent, though. She nodded distantly, and walked back into her house without saying another word.

Owen closed the trunk and hopped back in the driver's seat.

"I'll take the back this time," I said to Sarah, selfishly wanting to be the one to sit with the dog. Sarah nodded at me and we got into Luke's car.

"It smells like weed in here," Sarah complained as she closed the passenger door.

"Yeah, that's what months of hotboxing before concerts will do," Owen said. "Let's see if this starts." He turned the key in the ignition of Luke's old car.

I felt as much as heard the rumble of the engine.

"Full tank of gas," Owen announced.

I examined the interior of Luke's car. Rowdy sat next to me on a large patch of duct tape used to hold the seat cushion together. His tail was still wagging.

"Check this out," Owen said, holding up a cassette tape that he had pulled from off the dashboard. He read the words written on the label: "'Songs for the Road.'" He inserted the tape. "If we don't break down," he muttered sarcastically.

He pressed "Play" and Luke's favorite song played loudly.

"It sounds like he recorded this off the radio," Sarah stated, referencing the poor quality of the music.

"Well, where are we headed?"

Sarah set her phone down so that Owen could see the screen. She didn't speak; she appeared lost in the familiar guitar chords of Luke's song.

As Owen drove, I rested my hand on the soft puppy next to me and gazed out the window. As I listened to Luke's song, I felt tears forming in my eyes.

We drove along with only the sounds of the music. My mind flooded with memories of Luke and me as kids – playing together, climbing trees, and enjoying recess in grade school. Sarah looked over her seat at me with a consoling expression and sympathetic eyes. She was holding something that she passed to me. I examined the little photograph I now was holding. It was a picture of Luke and me when we were ten playing on his trampoline. My eyes welled with more tears when I read the caption: Be Childish.

Seeing the glove compartment open on Sarah's knees, I glanced back down at the photograph. Despite my tears, I chuckled.

"We were so proud of the sport we had

invented," I explained to them in a mix of laughter and tears. "Trampoline Basketball." Overcome with the humorous recollection, I added with a laugh, "Mostly we just got hit in the face."

Owen and Sarah laughed, too. I wiped the tears out of my eyes as Luke's song faded to its end. Before the moment could linger, my sentiment was sabotaged by the next track. Dominating our attention, the booming new sound was completely opposite from the previous.

"Alright, LUKE!" Owen yelled as he cranked up the volume to a ridiculous rap song.

We all started laughing as the heavy bass vibrated Luke's car. Owen and Sarah began dancing absurdly in their seats as the rap lyrics blared. Owen was doing some horrible pelvic thrust in time with the music like he was humping the base of the steering wheel; Sarah had her hands up in the air with her wrists pressed together, swaying back and forth. The creatively profane lyrics continued, and I couldn't help but laugh at the two of them. Owen and Sarah stared intensely into each other's eyes as they lip-synched the chorus. Rowdy was jumping on me, riled by all the commotion.

"Rowdy's dancing, too!" I yelled to them over the bass, and we all started laughing.

The song ended. Owen turned down the volume, and a less-intrusive tune served as background music. We followed the directions on Sarah's phone.

Eventually, Owen had to flip the tape over. I

enjoyed listening to the songs Luke had put on his mixtape, and wondered where he was taking us. As we drove, I considered that this must really mean the end of our journey. I had received my picture. Before I was the only one who hadn't. And I wasn't sure how to feel. There were so many more complexities to emotions than I had realized before all of this. How is it that the people we love the most can bring us the most pain?

As the current song came to an end there was only irritating static on the tape.

"I hope you understand why," Luke said softly. Slowly, I comprehended who had spoken.

Owen slammed on the brakes. Tires screeched behind us as we were nearly rear-ended. White-faced, he stared down at the cassette player. The tape had ended. Cars behind us honked as Owen shook his head, trying to shake off his surprise.

"Was that Luke just now, on the tape?" he asked, still stopped on the road.

My heart was beating rapidly as Sarah rewound the tape, and the three of us listened again to the sound of our dead friend's voice. I felt the hair on the back of my neck stand on end.

"Enough games!" Owen shouted in anger. He was breathing heavily with his hand on his chest.

"Pull over for a second," Sarah commanded him, taking note of the cars behind us.

Owen maneuvered the car to the side of the road.

"What the hell was that?" Owen asked. "Does

he think this is funny?" Owen's voice got louder with each word, and I could tell he was about to lose it.

"He just wants us to understand," I defended, even though I felt equally disturbed. Even amidst all our confusion, this adventure had proven one thing to me – it wasn't usually wise for us all to express the same emotion simultaneously.

"Well, I *don't* understand! I don't understand any of this. What a fucking hypocrite! End your life, but tell your friends how to live theirs. And what's most messed up is that he was probably enjoying putting all this together." Owen was crying now.

Sarah placed her hand on his shoulder.

"Don't touch me!" Owen yelled, deflecting her arm with his elbow.

Sarah withdrew her hand as though by reflex, and her eyes clouded with tears.

"Why is there such a thing as death?" Owen whimpered.

The sound of Owen's voice bothered me; he sounded like a little boy. This is not the kind of childish Luke wanted us to be, I thought.

"I think you're taking this the wrong way. I don't think he's playing with us. I think he did this to help us somehow."

And yet, in a strange way, I felt like we were back to the start; like we had relapsed or something. Once again, I felt the same level of confusion and lack of control as I had on our way to Eldorado National Forest.

"It's helping me," Sarah said quietly. "I mean, I

think I do understand. I understand the notes and the photographs." She paused. "But I don't understand his journal, or the paintings really. I don't fully understand Luke's mind. I mean, a part of me doesn't really want to. I get why he did this," she said gesturing around us. "But I don't understand why he killed himself."

"Because he's *selfish*!" Owen snapped back at her and whimpered as he cried, "Suicide is selfish."

"No it isn't!" I yelled at him. His statement had struck a nerve.

"Fuck off, Eric!"

His words stung, and I watched as Sarah reached across the seat and slapped him hard across the face.

"Stop talking!" she yelled, pounding his thigh with a clenched fist. "Just both of you *stop*!"

I heard Owen make a shaking exhale and touch his face as his eyes glistened with tears.

"Oh, my God," Sarah said. "I didn't mean to hit you that hard."

There was a red mark on the side of Owen's face and little scratches of blood from Sarah's fingernails.

"I'm sorry."

Everyone was quiet. I listened to the sounds of the traffic rushing by.

"I don't think suicide is selfish," I began, not caring whether it was appropriate to continue talking. It was my turn to say something.

Neither of them spoke.

"Saying it's selfish will just make sick people

feel worse. It'll just make them want to end their lives even more, to escape. I don't think Luke had any choice about feeling the way he did. I mean, I think he had a choice to get help or not – and that he should have. And I think he had a choice to ultimately go through with it – which he shouldn't have. But I don't think he was selfish. Even if he hurt us by what he did, he was hurting more. How can someone just insist that it's selfish and do nothing more, yet still expect someone to live in agony? That's what's selfish."

Sarah and Owen remained quiet.

"It's just that..." Owen was the first to break the silence. "I just can't stop thinking this horrible thought," Owen struggled. "I keep thinking that there must have been a time while doing all this that Luke thought, 'Well, the only thing left to do now is hang myself.'"

I felt the car shake slightly from the speed of passing vehicles.

"Let's keep going," Sarah suggested. "Do you want me to drive?"

"Yeah," Owen replied quietly.

Sarah waited for a pause in the traffic and then got out of the car and walked around to the driver's side. Owen scooted across the seats. Sarah got us back up to speed on the highway.

"I'm sorry I swore at you, Eric," Owen said after a while.

"I'm over it," I joked in reply.

Owen rested his face on the cushioned back of

his seat and looked over at Rowdy. He limply placed his hand out in an attempt to pet him, but Rowdy kept licking it.

"That tickles," he said, smiling weakly. "Who's a good dog?" Owen sat up a bit in his seat and spoke now in a high-pitched voice as he continued to confirm and reaffirm that it was, indeed, Rowdy who was a good dog. "I wish they allowed pets in the dorms," Owen said dreamily. "So, he's going to stay with your parents? When this is all over?"

"Hopefully," I replied. "But we can all share him. You know, take turns caring for him."

"That would be nice," Owen said.

"Of course," Sarah stated from the driver's seat, glancing back down at her phone. "How did I not see this before? Luke's taking us to the ocean."

My first glimpse of the Pacific appeared through the windshield. Owen read aloud the sign that we drove past, "Point Reyes National Seashore."

It wasn't long before we found ourselves parked beside a beach. We all got out of the car. I grabbed Rowdy's leash from the back and struggled to attach it to the overly excited dog's collar. Owen and I followed behind Sarah, but Rowdy strained to lead.

"You've got quite the strength for a puppy," I hollered above the sound of the waves, as Rowdy pulled me forward.

We followed Sarah diagonally down the sandy beach to a rocky point at its edge. The smooth sand was replaced now with flat, layered rocks. It became steeper as we attempted to traverse this unused section of the beach. Gnarled roots formed the eroded dirt wall that we now traveled alongside. Sarah held onto one of the protruding roots to keep herself steady as she examined her phone. She changed direction, and we walked to the edge of the ocean.

"Really?" Sarah said in an odd voice. "It's fifteen feet ahead of us," she concluded, stopping in her tracks and looking forward just as the waves reached their end right before our shoes. "We're going to need swimsuits."

Chapter 10
The Only Thing Left to Do

We ran back to the car and drove to the nearest store. The cashier took forever, slowly scanning the swimsuits and the towels and the goggles we had grabbed.

"Rowdy peed," I announced as we climbed back into the vehicle.

"And that's why we're driving Luke's car," Owen stated plainly.

Sarah started driving back toward the beach.

"Shit," Sarah cursed as raindrops began collecting on the windshield. She turned on the windshield wipers as dark, gray clouds advanced to dominate the sky.

"You've got to be kidding me," Owen sighed, peering out the passenger window. "I guess Luke's planning didn't take everything into account."

"We can still do this," Sarah said. "A little rain never hurt anybody." It started raining harder. "You know, I'm thinking about getting a tattoo," Sarah continued, ignoring the growing storm.

"Yeah, of what?" Owen asked.

"Those first coordinates," she answered, looking over at him. "I mean…this," she continued, focusing on the road as she drove on. "This experience is going to stay with me forever. I'm glad for it in a way. Luke's coordinates showed me the stars, and the world, and the ocean."

The beach came into view ahead of us.

"And you know what? I think I really do understand." Sarah framed her voice calmly as she dared to revisit our previous conversation. "I mean, I think I do get it," she asserted with a nod of her head. "I think he wanted to make an impact – a positive one. And despite the circumstances, I think his message is about truly living, and about change mattering."

I moved my gaze to Owen. He was staring at Sarah.

"You're probably right," he replied. "Maybe this is all about appreciating things, like *really* appreciating them. And maybe Luke wanted us to do what he couldn't, or at least *thought* he couldn't. Maybe he used this as a way of being remembered, too. I mean...he certainly won't be forgotten."

Their words helped me if only by the thought of Luke feeling understood. If only by evoking that indescribable joy Luke would feel in having someone say, "yes, I do know what you mean" even if he, himself, wasn't sure he had conveyed some philosophical sentiment clearly. Their words helped me if only by the thought of Luke being at peace knowing he had succeeded in his attempt to explain something so intimate, so personal, so challenging, and so potentially upsetting – something that words so easily fall short of capturing. And by the thought of his being accepted. Being validated. And perhaps most of all, their words helped me know Luke's soul survives in the places he's hidden it and the impacts he's made. I considered everything Luke had set into motion. All the new beginnings he had created, even if started by an ending. Luke had arranged to outlive his death…and somehow he had managed even to outlive his life.

We pulled alongside the vacant beach. The three of us struggled to change into our swimsuits in the car, using the towels for attempted privacy.

"No peeking, boys," Sarah said flirtatiously as she pulled off her shirt and slipped on the top of her bikini.

"Rowdy's peeking," Owen joked in an envious tone.

"Wait here, boy," I said to Rowdy as we got out of the car.

The wind had picked up. Sarah shielded her phone from the rain with the corner of her flapping towel as she led the way back to the point. The waves were rolling in with greater force now; they crashed over the flat rocks. Sarah wrapped her phone in her towel and we weighed all our towels down with broken chunks of stone. We stood there, each waiting for the other. None of us wanted to be the first to enter the cold ocean.

"Let's go," Owen dared as he walked into the water. "Ready, boys?" he asked, looking down at his swim trunks as he allowed the water level to creep above them. His expression was one of sheer agony as he continued further in.

"Oh, come on," Sarah said, rolling her eyes

before marching out a ways and diving in next to him.

I stepped to the edge.

"Just how cold is it?" I asked.

Sarah splashed me in response. "That cold."

I stuck my tongue out at her.

"You're being childish," Sarah said to me, laughing.

I ran in after them. We waded out further and felt the beginning of a sudden slope. Together, we put on our goggles and submerged.

Despite the rain, I could clearly see my underwater surroundings. We propelled ourselves downward until we could pat the sandy floor of the ocean. We weren't having any luck and I was running out of air. I looked around and found the others already had returned to the surface. I swam to join them, and gasped for air as I broke through the watery barrier.

"Did you guys see anything?"

They shook their heads.

"Let's keep trying."

We all breathed deeply together before lowering our bodies back into the depths. Then I saw it!

Waving from the sand was a green ribbon easily mistaken for seaweed. But now that I recognized it, it was unmistakable. Moving my arms around rapidly, I got my friends' attention. They swam over to me and I pointed. Their eyes widened over their puffed cheeks. Together, we took hold of the ribbon and pulled upward. Another camo-colored capsule appeared and sent up a cloud of sand as it was dislodged from its watery hiding spot. Tucking the container under my arm, I swam back to the surface. There, we tread water and tried to catch our breath.

Eventually, we swam back to the shallow point near the rocky side of the beach and made our way back to the shore. The rain was letting up and a few of the sun's rays broke through the clouds as it descended nearer to the horizon. The summer day was coming to an end.

In the drizzling rain, we stood on the beach together. I unscrewed the top of the container and found the capsule contained only one thing: a small note. I removed it, set the container down, and held the note so that the three of us could read what was written on the front.

You're not done searching. There's more to find. Just look out ahead of you.

Keep living, keep being kind, keep having adventures, keep making memories, keep being friends, keep having fun, keep being childish.

And keep searching,
Luke Leary

I dropped my hand to my side, with the note held tightly between my fingers. Owen placed his arm over Sarah's shoulder, and my other hand rested on Sarah's back. We stood there together. The three of us. On the beach in the rain. Looking out over the ocean at sunset.

www.ingramcontent.com/pod-product-compliance
Lightning Source LLC
Chambersburg PA
CBHW020147180626
46810CB00004B/1781